Paradise End

Paradise End

ELIZABETH LAIRD

MACMILLAN CHILDREN'S BOOKS

First published 2004 by Macmillan Children's Books
a division of Macmillan Publishers Limited
20 New Wharf Road, London N1 9RR
Basingstoke and Oxford
Associated companies throughout the world
www.panmacmillan.com

ISBN 0 333 98095 6

1 3 5 7 9 8 6 4 2

A CIP catalogue record for this book is available from
the British Library.

Typeset by Intype Libra Ltd
Printed and bound in Great Britain
by Mackays of Chatham plc, Kent

For Ashleigh

1

'What's it going to be, Lauren, a slap or a kick? Or are you going to move that stuff and shut that noise up and let me get on with my tap?'

That's me talking to my little sister, and don't feel sorry for her. Listen to the next bit.

'Mum!' shrieks Lauren. 'Carly's hitting me! Mum! It's not fair!'

'I am not hitting you, you little slug.' I'm so irritated my face is sweating now. 'But I will if you don't shut up. At *once*.'

It's too late. The door opens and Mum's there.

'Carly, not again.' She sounds as if she's pulled me off Lauren six times in the last hour, which she hasn't. 'Can't you two play nicely together for once?'

'Excuse me.' I am as cold as ice. 'I am not *playing*. I do not *play*. I'm trying to practise my steps, which, if you will remember, Mrs Litvinov asked me to do every day. And I never touched Lauren. She's such a little liar, she wouldn't know the truth if it wore a bright-green costume and jumped out of her breakfast cereal.'

I'm quite pleased with that, but it doesn't impress Mum. She's hugging Lauren now, who is snivelling (or pretending to) and looking triumphantly out at me over Mum's arm.

'I've had it up to here with you, madam.' Mum's shaking her forefinger at me, and it's so unfair that I kick the leg of my bed and make a nasty scuff mark on my beautiful right tap shoe.

Then she takes Lauren out of the room, and I know she's going to give the little beast a drink and a biscuit in the nice cosy kitchen. And my head's fizzing with fury, and my fists are itching to punch someone, and my feet are twitching with frustration. So then I fling open the window and I turn up the music (I don't care what the old misery next door thinks) and I start my tap.

Clickety clack, clickety clack, clickety clickety clack clack clack.

I'm good today. All that anger's given me energy. The buzz thrills from my brain clean down my spine and through my legs into my dancing feet, and they're going strong, tapping and clicking on the floorboards, forwards and backwards, every stroke perfect, just this once.

Wish Mrs Litvinov could see me now, I'm thinking. I'd be up for the display. But then the door crashes open and it's Mum again. She storms over to the window, slams it shut, marches to the stereo and switches it off.

'You *know* poor old Mavis next door is poorly and sleeps in the afternoon,' she rages. 'How can you be so inconsiderate?'

'Easily,' I say, 'when people don't give any consideration to me. All I ask – *all* I ask – is a bit of space to practise in.' I know I've been mean to Misery Mavis so I rush on. 'Look at the floor, Mum. Look at it. The minute I start, what does Lauren do? Spreads her rubbishy Barbie gear all over it, and screams the house down if I dance within five miles of it. Anyway, for your information, I didn't hit her. I told you before. She's a lying little toad.'

Mum heaves a sigh.

'It's only till September. When Sam goes off to college you'll get your own room. I know it's not easy, Carly, sharing a bedroom when you're nearly fourteen, but you could at least try to be nice to Lauren. After all, she's only . . .'

'Eight years old. Lauren's age is something I know, Mum, although thanks for reminding me. Why do I keep thinking she's only four? Or three? Barbie dolls. I mean, give me a break.'

And I lash out at all those revolting little glitzy dresses and sparkly pink miniature handbags and tiny sequinned sweaters with a sweep and a click-clack of my black shoe, and now there's a decent empty space on the floor, and I can get started again, if anyone will let me, on my practice.

'I'll keep the volume down, promise,' I say, reaching for the button on the stereo. 'Please, Mum. I've got to get on. Mrs Litvinov's selecting for the display this Saturday. She says I'm up for it, if I get my brushes right.'

'Saturday. Yes.' Mum takes a deep breath as if she's about to get something off her chest, but she doesn't get the chance because Lauren's poked her weaselly little face out from behind her.

'I'm coming with you on Saturday,' she says. 'Mum says I can. I'm starting in the junior class with Miss Tideswell. We're going to buy the shoes at Quicksteps after school on Friday. Mum says we can.'

I honestly can't remember what happened next. That's the thing about anger, fury, rage – call it what you like. It wipes your mind of everything else. I got that wild feeling in my head, and I said things and yelled and threw stuff.

And then I'd thrown off my tap shoes, and wrenched on my trainers and was out of the house, out in the street, just needing to be on my own, with space round me, and time to let the heat go off, and the jangling nerves all over my body start to calm down.

I didn't care where I was going. I ran up the road, past poor old Mavis's and all the other boring semis at the crummy end of our village, desperate to get away.

I don't know about you, but for me, if I'm angry, the best thing is to go off somewhere, to get right away and cool my head. I need to be on my own. That's the problem with rushing out of the house. Anyone seeing me storming up the road that afternoon, muttering to myself and waving my arms around, would have thought I was a total fruitcake. They'd have called for an ambulance, probably.

But by the time I was halfway up the hill I was over the worst of it. I usually do calm down quite quickly, as a matter of fact. So when I reached the top, I was able to forget about Mum and Lauren and Miss Tideswell for a moment, and look through the bars of the old-fashioned wrought-iron gates, which stand like sentries at the top of our street, and are so tall you can see them from right down the bottom of the hill.

I've done that – looked through those gates, I mean – since I was a baby in my pushchair, before I could walk and long before I could spell out the words carved into

4

the massive gate pillars: 'Paradise' on the left one, and 'End' on the right.

How can I describe Paradise End to you? Words mightn't be enough. If I call it a stately home, you'll think of something huge, like a palace or a castle. If I call it a big house, you'll probably imagine something too small and ordinary. Well then. Paradise End is a stately home, but a little one.

Once, it must have stood in lonely splendour on the crown of the hill, with the village tucked away in the valley bottom below. But the village grew and grew, and modern estates like ours crept up the hill till they reached all the way to the gates.

The house is about 200 years old, and it's got a big front door in the middle, between a couple of long, elegant windows, and then the walls bulge out on each side to make two large bays, with three long windows in each one. There are about nine windows running along the upstairs floor, and they're a bit shorter than the ones below.

That doesn't tell you much, does it? I'd like you to do what I've always done, hold the bars and peer round to the right of the house, to glimpse what's obviously the end of a stone terrace going along the side, and the long lawn that slopes away from it towards a fringe of old giant beech trees, and then look left to the row of garages running alongside the drive near the gates. They must have been stables once, I suppose. There are little windows sticking out of the roof above, because there are flats up there. But even if you can imagine that, it's not enough. It doesn't tell you about the feel of the place, its mystery and beauty and strength. It doesn't tell you that Paradise End is the sort of place that starts you making up stories in your head, that makes you stop and look and dream.

It was almost better a few years ago, when it was no more than a wreck. There were weeds shooting up out of the drive running up to the front door, and bushes sprouting out of the roof. The lawn was like a field, with really long grass, and the flower-beds had disappeared. It had a quiet, old, romantic, dreamy look to it then.

A rich old miser was supposed to have lived there once. People said he'd quarrelled with everyone and become a hermit in the end. We used to make up stories about him to scare the infants. We'd tell them he'd murdered his wife and eaten his kids and shot at the postman with a big shotgun.

Last summer, though, everything changed. The padlock came off the gates and workmen moved in. They painted all the ironwork a shiny black, and the drive was cleaned up with new gravel, all sharp and glittery. The grass was a lawn again and the flower-beds were weeded. The house was a dazzling white now, and there were a couple of miniature trees in white tubs, one on each side of the front door, standing to attention like little soldiers. The sun sparkled on the freshly washed windows, and you could see that there were new curtains inside, thick heavy ones, tied back with fancy ropes.

You might think that this is a bit weird of me, but in my heart of hearts I've always dreamed about Paradise End, and in my dreams it always belongs to me and I'm the mistress of it all. When I was younger, I used to imagine that I'd been swapped at birth, or found by my parents in

6

a Moses basket, and that one day someone would knock at our front door and announce that I was the rightful owner of Paradise End, and hand me a silver key on a velvet cushion.

I'm more realistic now. A bit more anyway. I know that Mum's my mum, and Dad's my dad and that in this life no one hands you anything on a plate. In my dream it's me who makes things happen. I can see myself from the outside. I'm dancing somewhere in the open and the world's most famous impressario drives past and sees me, just by chance, and he stops his chauffeur and tells me I'm the greatest. Then he whisks me off to Hollywood and stardom. I come back in a blaze of diamonds and buy Paradise End. Only then, when it's truly mine, do I open the front door and walk inside and take possession of the rooms one by one, and discover all that's inside them.

I loved that part, imagining the rooms and all the things in them. And sometimes I played out little scenes in my head, like there were vanloads of flowers arriving at the front door, sent by all my fans, or I was kindly letting the most stuck-up girls from my class at school come to tea, or I was on the phone saying, 'No, Lauren, you certainly cannot bring Francine and Darren to play here, and if I ever catch you hanging round my gates again I'll get the butler and the footman and the chauffeur and the housekeeper and the dogs on to you so fast you won't know what's hit you.'

Anyway, as I stood there that afternoon, I was imagining myself giving a ball, wearing a fabulous ball-gown, and sweeping down the grand staircase, into the arms of the most stunning man in the world, while Lauren was carried away kicking and screaming down the drive. That made me feel a bit better, and I turned away to walk down Church Lane (it runs down to the left of the big gates along the wall of Paradise End into the old, middle part of the village).

I'll go for a really long walk, I thought. And I won't get home for hours and hours. Mum'll get dead worried and maybe she'll realize for once how upset I am.

And then the most amazing thing happened. I'd only gone a couple of steps, when a shy voice behind me said, 'Hi.'

I looked round, but I couldn't see anyone, so I walked on, but then the same voice said, 'Hello, I'm in here.'

Then I saw her. There was a girl standing inside the big gates, holding a tennis racket in one hand and one of the uprights of the gate in the other. She was about the same height as me, and slim with long, honey-coloured hair. She was wearing jeans and a tight-fitting pink top, so I could see she was even flatter than me in front, if such a thing is possible, though I guess we were the same age.

'Sorry,' she said, sounding shyer than ever. 'My tennis ball's gone under that red car. You couldn't fish it out for me, could you? It's such a pain opening the gates. They always shut on me and lock me out.'

I just stood and stared. She'd given me an awful shock. I suddenly saw, painfully clearly, how silly all my dreams had been. For the first time, I suppose, I realized that Paradise End must belong to someone else. It must have real owners, real people, who had a right to live there.

I was all set to hate the girl straight off, especially when the poshness of her voice had started to sink in. No one I

8

knew, no one round our estate or at my school, ever sounded like she did. I thought she must be taking the mickey, and I was just about to say, 'Sorry, I haven't got time. I'm in a hurry,' when I noticed the anxious crease in her forehead, and saw her eyes.

I'd never seen eyes that colour before. They weren't either blue or green, but somewhere in the middle. You see that colour sometimes when shallow sea-water runs over white sand, or when the sky is very clear on a winter afternoon. As a matter of fact, they were the most extra-ordinary eyes I'd ever seen. They only looked at me, though, for a moment, before she dropped them from mine, but I'd seen a sort of pleading in them.

'Which red car?' I said. 'There are hundreds out here.'

'That one.'

She pointed her racket towards a lumbering old Toyota, the longest and widest car in the street, as luck would have it.

I bent down. The ball was new and bright yellow, so I saw it at once, lodged behind the back wheel. There was another one further in, harder to reach. I had to get down on my hands and knees and stretch my arm out as far as it would go. I dislodged the ball with my fingertips and it rolled towards the other one by the back wheel. I pulled myself back from under the car, and picked them both up.

'Two of them,' I said. 'Are they both yours?'

She put her hand through the bars and I put the balls into it.

'I expect so. I lose hundreds when I'm practising my backhand. You are an angel.'

We stood there awkwardly, looking at each other, and I

remember thinking right then that we couldn't have been more different. She was blonde and sleek, perfectly groomed, her clothes fitting like a skin, her hair cut by a genius, her voice as posh as a princess's. I'm tall too, but I'm all elbows and knees, Mum says, bony and skinny, and my short black hair sticks out over my ears and forehead in spikes whatever I do to it. If I wear tights, they always get holes in them. If I wear a top tucked into my jeans, it always comes flying out. I was ready to hate her again, partly for looking as if she could go through a car wash and come out the other side as perfect as when she went in, but mostly because she was living in my dream, my Paradise End.

I said, 'OK then. Bye,' and I started to move away.

'Bye,' she said softly, but then, when I'd only gone about five steps, she called out, 'You wouldn't like a game of tennis, would you? It's hopeless trying to practise on one's own.'

I stopped and turned back. The meaning of what she'd said, the idea that I might actually be able to walk through those gates, that had been shut against me all my life, was making my heart jump about inside my chest.

'I'm useless at tennis,' I said, feeling breathless. 'I always whack the balls into the net when we play at school.'

She laughed awkwardly.

'Oh. Do you – I mean, would you like to come and see the tennis court anyway? It might inspire you or some-thing.'

I'd never thought I was much good at reading people's minds, and I was all taken up with my own feelings, but I could tell that she was lonely. It stuck out a mile. She might have been grand, and rich, and have brilliant clothes, but the cards weren't all stacked on her side. I had something she wanted, that I could give or keep back: company.

'OK,' I said, trying to sound casual. 'Just for a bit. I can't stay long though.'

Then she pressed a hidden button on the inside of one of the pillars, and the gates swung open, and I walked through them, into her life.

2

It was the weirdest thing I'd ever done, walking up the gravel drive towards the front of Paradise End. Later, when my dream of the house had faded and I knew the real one so well, my love for it almost scared me, but that day I was nervous more than anything else. The blank windows of the long facade looked down like disapproving eyes, and I was terrified that the door would open, and someone would come out and shout at me, to send me packing like a naughty child.

I thought we were about to go in through the front door, but the girl veered off to the right before we reached the pillars and the tubs, with their little sentry trees. We went so close to the long windows that I wanted to creep past on tiptoe, like a trespasser, in case someone was watching us from inside. I had to make myself walk normally.

We reached the corner of the house and went round it on to the terrace. It was very long, and was made of soft old stone. A flight of wide stone steps swept down from the terrace to acres of lawn below. Masses of brightly coloured flowers spilled out of the flower-beds below the terrace. It was all a million times more beautiful than I'd ever imagined.

I couldn't help gasping.

'I didn't know it was so huge,' I said. 'You'd never guess it was like this from the outside. It's totally, totally amazing.'

She was holding a strand of her blonde hair, twisting it round in her fingers, watching me. I was afraid I'd sounded silly and gushy, like a tourist or something, so I tried to look bored.

'Terrible lot of work, keeping all this up,' I said grandly. 'Who cuts the grass? Your dad?'

'The gardeners do it,' she said carelessly.

A hot blush swept up my cheeks. I felt stupid, angry with her and furious with myself.

'Come on,' she said, dropping her hand from her hair. 'I'll show you the tennis court.'

She jumped down the terrace steps and didn't stop when she reached the bottom, but ran across the lawn with her hair streaming out behind her. I raced after her, glad not to have to talk, and we burst through the rim of trees and turned left behind the house. And I stopped dead and stared, and my mouth fell open in spite of myself.

It wasn't the tennis court I was looking at (which as far as I could see was just the usual sort), but the swimming pool in front of it. The glittering blue water stretched away to a kind of summer house at the far end, where there were basket-work chairs and sofas. There were bushes round the edge of the pool, so that it looked natural, as if it had started off as a formal kind of pond. The house was reflected in the water, and was a sharp, bright white, as perfect as a wedding cake.

'Wow,' was all I could say.

'Do you like it?' the girl said, looking at me with those sea-green eyes.

I couldn't read her expression. I was wary, afraid I'd say something else that would give her the chance to smile. I felt a spurt of resentment.

'Of course I like it,' I snapped. 'Who wouldn't? You wouldn't bother to ask if you lived in a three-bedroom semi like me.'

She blushed scarlet and tossed the hair off her face with a flick of her head.

I've embarrassed her, I thought. Good.

'Who does all this belong to then?' I said, feeling bolder. 'Your dad? The one who doesn't do any gardening?'

'No, it's my uncle's and my mother's.' Her voice sounded remote. 'Daddy lives in Argentina, in Buenos Aires. My parents are divorced.'

'Oh.'

I didn't know what to say. I felt like someone walking across a swamp on stepping stones. One false move and you're up to your neck in mud.

We stood in silence for a moment, then I realized what had been puzzling away at the back of my head.

'I don't get it,' I said. 'How come your tennis balls went out into the road? The gates are miles from here, right round the other side of the house.'

'You can't bounce balls off anything round here,' she said, looking embarrassed. 'It's easy at the front. The garage wall's brilliant for practice.'

She was still holding her tennis racket and she began to

swing it, as if she was practising her strokes. She didn't fool me though.

You weren't bothered about your tennis, I thought, feeling a sort of triumph. You were just hanging about, waiting for someone to come past who you could talk to.

The thought made me feel more confident.

'I'd better be going,' I said, looking at my watch.

'Why? You're not in a hurry, are you?' She spoke quickly, as if she was looking for something to say, so that she could keep me there.

'No.' I stopped. I wanted to say something that would impress her, but I couldn't think of anything. 'I was only going for a bit of a walk.'

'A walk? Where to?'

'I don't know. Through the village. Down to the river maybe.'

She looked envious.

'You are lucky. No one ever lets me go out on my own. I've never gone for walks. I've never been able to explore at all.'

I stared at her. I know every tree, every hedge and every fence-post round here. If you put me down a mile from our house in any direction I'd walk straight home, I reckon, just by feeling the way with my toes.

I shrugged.

'You haven't missed much. Canningtree's not exactly the trendiest place in the whole wide world.'

I looked at my watch again. Time had whizzed past. I'd wanted Mum to get worried, but I hadn't wanted her to get into a frenzy and start phoning the hospital. I began to walk back round the house towards the terrace that would take me out to the front again. She walked beside me. I heard her take a deep breath, then she said. 'Could – I mean, can I come to your house some time?'

Awful snapshots flashed through my head – our scrubby little patch of garden with the broken plastic climbing frame and Dad's underpants hanging on the washing-line, Sam's smelly trainers on the mat inside the back door, Mum's sharp voice telling everyone to damn well come and eat their supper before it froze right over, Lauren's awful baby-doll stuff scattered all over our bedroom floor.

'I dunno. Sometime maybe,' I said.

We reached the gates. I looked at the back of the pillar for the button that would open them.

'Hey,' said the girl, 'I never asked your name.'

It was funny, but at that moment I almost didn't want to tell her. I had a feeling that if I didn't we'd never see each other again, and it might be better, that we both ought to stay in our own worlds and keep out of each other's hair. But she was smiling at me, waiting for me to answer, and there were these dimples in her cheeks, and she looked so friendly and hopeful that I suddenly knew I liked her. She wasn't one bit like the usual people I went around with, but I wanted her to be my friend. I really, really did.

'It's Carol Mary McQuarrie,' I said. 'You can call me Carly, but not Mac. I hate Mac. What's yours?'

'Anastasia.'

'Ana what?'

'Actually, it's Anastasia Lucille Braithwaite Krukovsky.'

She looked almost defiant for a moment, and I could see she was watching for my reaction. I was impressed, to

16

be honest, but I'd have died rather than show it. I suppose I was trying to think of something else to say, to cut her down to size, but I didn't need to, because she did it to herself. She shrank right down again, in front of my eyes, and now her look was questioning and anxious, as if she was afraid I was annoyed with her.

'You can call me Tia,' she said a bit nervously, as if she was trying to make a joke of it and didn't quite know how I'd take it. 'But not Annie. I can't abide Annie.'

I smiled at that, and she smiled back, and we were both grinning at each other full on as the gates swung open.

'I've got to go, really,' I said, 'or Mum'll do a total number on me.'

'OK,' she said as the gates swung shut behind me. 'Awfully nice to have met you, Carly.'

'Yes,' I said. 'You too, Tia.'

I raced home. I'd forgotten about the row with Mum and Lauren. I was just dying to tell someone about Paradise End and Tia.

Mum was waiting for me, her face like a thundercloud.

'Don't you dare do that to me again, ever,' she burst out, her cheeks going bright red as I came in through the back door. 'Running out on me like that. I've been worried sick. Had visions of you under a car, lost, attacked . . .'

She stopped, and I thought she was going to cry. I felt mean.

'Sorry, Mum.' I wanted to whip up a bit of the anger I'd felt before, to make her see why I'd had to rush out, but I couldn't feel it any more.

'Where have you *been*?' her voice came out as a wail.

Lauren had appeared now. Trust her to shove her nose in.

'We thought you'd been got by a pervert,' she said, sounding disappointed.

I ignored her.

'I only went for a walk,' I said.

It was funny. I'd been bursting to tell Mum everything a minute ago, but now I didn't want to. Back in our kitchen, with the untidy heap of ironing on the table, and all the dirty dishes heaped up on the draining board, Paradise End seemed as distant as the moon.

'I know where you went,' Lauren said spitefully. 'You went down by the river, where Mum said not to go.'

She can always do it to me, Lauren can. She can always wind me up. I hadn't been able to feel angry a moment before, when I'd almost wanted to, but now I could feel myself start to boil.

'Get her out of here, Mum,' I pleaded. 'Tell her to shut it.'

To my surprise, Mum did turn on Lauren.

'That was quite unnecessary,' she said. 'Go and tidy up the mess you've made in the sitting room.'

Lauren sidled towards the kitchen door, then stopped.

'Go on,' Mum said, losing interest in her.

Lauren went slowly out through the door, but I knew she was standing in the hall, listening. I didn't care any more. I knew I'd won that round.

Mum was putting the kettle on.

'Carly, you know I've told you, time and again, that it's not safe by the river. Janice Harding got flashed there last year, and those two girls from the holiday cottages . . .'

That did it.

'Mum!' I felt like exploding. 'Read my lips: I – did – not go to the river.' I stopped, trying to shake my fury off. 'Why do you always listen to Lauren? Spiteful little cat. She never, never stops stirring it.' I heard a shuffling noise outside the door and raised my voice. 'Go on, you. You heard Mum. Go and tidy up your crappy stuff and stop listening to other people's conversations,' and I marched over to the door and slammed it shut.

Mum put tea bags into a couple of mugs.

'Where did you go then, love?' she said, and she just sounded interested, not angry any more, so I gave in and sat down at the table.

'I went to Paradise End,' I said.

She was pouring boiling water into the mugs, but her head jerked up and she frowned at me. I was afraid the water would spill and burn her hands.

'What do you mean? Carly, you didn't try to climb in over the wall?'

'What?' I couldn't believe she'd said that. 'Have you looked at the wall, Mum? It's about ninety metres high and there's broken glass all along the top. Look at my hands. No cuts. No scratches. OK?'

'Sorry.' She fished the tea bags out of the mugs, slopped some milk into them, pushed one over to my side of the table and sat down opposite me, the mug between her hands. 'What happened then?'

'Well, when I went up the road, I didn't care where I was going. I was so furious.'

'Yes, I know.' She nodded. 'I'm sorry. I should have warned you about Lauren going to Miss Tideswell's class. I knew you'd be upset. I suppose I was putting it off.'

She reached into the cupboard behind her and pulled out a packet of biscuits. She took one and started nibbling it round the edges. My mum's thick round the middle, frankly, and a bit short, with a couple of double chins. She knows she ought to resist biscuits. She can't, but she eats them slowly. It's as if she thinks her stomach won't notice if she only sends tiny bits down at a time.

'Go on,' she said, offering the packet to me.

'Anyway,' I went on, 'when I was passing the gates, this girl called out from inside. Asked me to get her tennis balls out from under the car for her.'

Mum looked interested.

'I thought someone must have moved in. I've seen cars going in and out recently.'

'Yes, well they have. Anyway, we got talking. She was really nice. She asked me in to look at the tennis court they've got in there, so I did. It's so brilliant. It's a totally, totally incredible place. She talks posh, but she wasn't a bit grand, honestly. I thought she was kind of lonely. I really liked her. I mean, she's really, really nice.'

I was going over the top, I know, but I didn't want Mum to get the wrong idea about Tia. She's fussy about where she lets me go and who she lets me see. I wanted to get her on to Tia's side. It didn't work. She was frowning.

'You mean you went in there? On your own? How many times have I told you—'

'Not to go to strange places, get into cars, talk to weirdos, wander down dark lanes in the middle of the night shouting, "Come here all you mad murderers and strangle me." I know, Mum. But Tia's my age, and—'

'What did you call her?'

'Tia. Her real name's Anastasia Lucille something something.'

'Very fancy,' Mum said drily, but I could see she was curious. She leaned forward and took another biscuit. 'What's the house like inside? I've always wanted to see it. They must have spent a fortune on it.'

'Oh, I didn't go in.' I wanted to tell her everything now. 'Just round the outside to the back. It's huge, Mum, the garden. You'd never believe how much space there is in there. And there's this swimming pool – it's unbelievable. I mean, it's really pretty, made to look like a lake, all wild, with bushes all round it.'

The door opened and Lauren marched back into the kitchen.

'I can't tidy up,' she said. 'I'm too hungry. I need a biscuit.'

She reached for the packet. I snatched it up and held it over her head.

'Say please.'

'Don't, Carly,' said Mum wearily. 'Just give her one.'

I lowered the packet slowly. Lauren grabbed it out of my hand.

'You're making it up about Paradise End,' she said, her mouth full of biscuit. 'There aren't any girls living there. Only a mad old miser.'

'You've been listening outside the door,' I said triumphantly. 'Little sneak.'

'No I haven't.' She was looking sideways at Mum

21

though. 'You talked so loud I could hear you in the sitting room where I was trying to concentrate on tidying up my stuff.'

Mum and I looked at each other and smiled. Lauren saw. She turned red and stamped her foot.

'It's true. There aren't any girls there. Darren told me, and he knows. This miser, he goes round with a gun, shooting at people. And he takes his clothes off in the day-time and shows you his willy. He's a pervert.'

'That'll do, Lauren,' Mum said sharply. 'I can't imagine where you get all these silly stories from. Old Joshua Braithwaite died years ago, seventy years at least. And there was nothing wrong with his mind. He'd have been a nicer person if he had been ill, probably. He made a for-tune out of coal-mining, working people like slaves. He bought Paradise End, furniture and all, from the family who'd always lived there, but he was too mean to spend a penny on it. His son took it on, and he was just as bad. A horrible man, by all accounts. His wife ran off and left him with twin babies. It must have been more than thirty or forty years ago. Where these mad-pervert stories come from I can't imagine. Have you tidied your stuff away yet? I'm going to give you five more minutes, and if you haven't finished by then there'll be trouble.'

She stood up, took our empty mugs and turned away to the sink. I waggled my head at Lauren, who stuck her tongue out at me.

I could tell she was seething with jealousy. It was great.

3

Saturday mornings always used to be the same. Up early. Hunt around for my dancing gear. Eat breakfast. Practise in the kitchen (not bad on the vinyl floor). Get sent away by Mum or Dad. Practise in my bedroom. Shout at Lauren for getting in the way. Noise wakes Sam, whose bedroom is next to ours. Get shouted at by Sam for waking him. Get some money off Mum. Rush to the bus stop opposite the war memorial. Trundle into Torminster. Arrive at the Wellesley Community Centre. Run up to Room Three.

'Ah there you are, Carly,' says Mrs Litvinov. 'Hope you're feeling energetic. We're going to *work* today.'

If anyone else tells me they're going to make me work, I slump down and feel bored, but I don't with Mrs Litvinov. She makes me want to *click* and *clack* and *bebop a do ba* till my rhythms are perfect and I can do a hundred wings on a roll. She's got to be the best teacher in the universe. (If ever I had to fill in a questionnaire on 'Who do you admire most in the world?' there'd be no problem for me. Mrs Litvinov would up there at Number One.)

That's how it *ought* to be on a Saturday morning. That's how it *used* to be, till the day when Lauren began in Miss Tideswell's class.

'Mum,' starts Lauren, while I'm rushing through my breakfast, 'can I go in the front seat, seeing it's my first time at tap and I'm really nervous?'

'In the front seat?' says Mum. She's still in her dressing gown and her hair's a bird's nest (that last perm was a mistake, in my view). 'Oh, you mean in the car? Look, darling, I know I said I'd take you, but I just can't. You'll have to go on the bus with Carly. If I don't get the washing done this morning there won't be a thing in this house for anyone to wear come Monday morning.'

'But you said!' whines Lauren. 'You promised!'

Dad looks up from behind his paper.

'The road's up anyway between here and Torminster,' he says. 'The queues will be backing right into the village. We've had to put someone on duty to sort out the traffic.'

I didn't explain this before, but my dad's a policeman. It's not the sort of thing you say straight off. Some people can be really funny about it.

'That's definitely it then,' says Mum. 'I'm not spending the whole of Saturday morning stuck in a jam. You and Carly will just have to go on your own.'

I shut my eyes. I can't trust myself to speak. Dad looks at his watch.

'I'd give yourselves an extra half hour at least if you don't want to be late.' He waggles his eyebrows at Lauren. 'Go on, fairy princess. Get your act together and buzz off. And don't forget your magic wand.'

Then he starts munching on another piece of toast.

I usually really love my dad. I mean, he's good-looking, tall, with great muscles and a neat haircut, and he even

24

looks quite hunky in his uniform, but when he calls Lauren his fairy princess, I want to kick his shins.

Lauren gives me a look. I can see she doesn't want to go by herself with me any more than I want to go with her. I have a micro-second flashback to my first tap class and how I had this mad urge to hide behind Mum, and an unusual feeling comes over me. It could be that I feel a sort of something like sympathy.

'Dadd-ee,' wheedles Lauren, 'couldn't you take us? Please? Ple-ease?'

'Can't,' says Dad, swilling his toast down with a slurp of tea. 'On duty. Got to be out Sturbridge way by half-past ten. You'll be all right. Twinkle-toes here will look after you.'

I scowl at him. Calling Lauren his fairy princess is bad enough, but calling me Twinkle-toes is the end.

So there it was. That was it. It was Lauren and me, on our own, going to tap, on the bus.

And for once, would you believe it, Lauren decided to be nice. She fetched her new tap shoes, wriggled into her skinny denim jacket, got her money off Mum and followed me out of the front door without a single wise-crack.

There was only one lapse. To get to the bus stop, we had to go up to Paradise End and turn left down Church Lane. I couldn't help slowing down a bit, looking out for Tia and remembering how I'd gone in through those gates a couple of days earlier, when Lauren says, in a really loud voice, 'That's where she lives then, is it, your friend, Tia? In there?'

'You know it is, Sneaky-ears,' I say. 'You were listening at the keyhole, remember?'

'Can't see her,' says Lauren, pretending to peer in through the gates.

'Well, you won't, will you?' I say, grabbing her by the sleeve and pulling her on. 'She's inside, waiting for her private tennis coach to come. She has her tennis lessons on a Saturday morning. Just her and him. He's an Olympic champion.'

Which was all my imagination, of course, but it might have been true.

It shut Lauren up anyway. She was as good as gold after that. She hardly said a word as we sat on the bus and it crawled slowly down the main road to Torminster. And when we got to the Wellesley Centre, in the middle of Torminster High Street, she actually took hold of my hand and held it, and I actually held hers back. I even squeezed it as we walked up the steps. And I didn't leave her in the front hall to find her own way, which I'd decided I was going to do, but took her over to Miss Tideswell's class in the annexe, and told Miss Tideswell she was my little sister, and she'd come to start with the beginners.

You won't believe this, but when I went to the door and looked back, and saw her standing by herself in the middle of the room, looking as if she wanted to die, I even blew her a kiss.

I must be going soft in the head.

Someone up there must have clocked that blown kiss, because I had my reward as soon as the lesson was over. Mrs Litvinov asked me stay behind.

'That was good, Carly,' she said, looking up from the notebook she'd been writing in. 'You've come on a mile since last term. I can tell you've been practising. I'm putting you down for the Black Shoes Display at the Performing Arts Festival.'

I had to stop myself squeaking out loud with triumph.

'There'll only be the three of you doing solo numbers,' Mrs Litvinov went on. 'Lizzie and Simone are doing hip-hop routines, quite straightforward, but I want you to work on a retro-jazz dance. Modern steps, lots of energy, plenty of technique, but in a classical style. Not easy, but we've got till the end of June, so there are two months to go. It means not missing a single Saturday morning for the rest of this term. There'll be extra practices on Wednesday evenings starting in June. Think you can commit to that?'

'Yes.' I was grinning like a clown from ear to ear.

'Good. There'll be your costume to sort out, of course. I'll have a note for you to take home next week. The display's going to be at the town hall. Wellesley won two medals last year. We're going to beat that this time, and you're one of my best hopes.'

Don't worry, Mrs Litvinov, I won't let you down, I said, but only in my head, because it would have sounded nerdy out loud.

Lauren was waiting for me outside. I could see at a glance that she'd got her bounce back and was her irritating cocky self all over again.

'Miss Tideswell says I've got excellent posture.' She was skipping along the edge of the kerbstone, close up to the cars, the way Mum always tells her she shouldn't. I wasn't

27

going to bother. 'She says I'm promising. Did she say you were promising on your very first day?'

'Look, there's our bus.' I grabbed her arm and made her run for it. I wasn't going to let Lauren spoil my triumph.

On the way home from the bus stop, when we passed Paradise End, I slowed down a bit, and looked in through the gates, but there was no sign of Tia. After we'd turned down into our street though, we heard the roar of a powerful engine, and a silver sports car swept past us. I looked back, and saw the gates of Paradise End swing slowly open and then shut behind it. It was too late then to see who was in the car, except that a man was driving it, a young man. I caught a glimpse of a headful of swept-back tawny hair, and saw a pair of black gloves on the steering wheel.

4

It was pouring all the next day, on the Sunday, and the following weekend Dad took us all down to the coast to visit his mum and his two old aunties. During the weekdays, of course, I was at school.

I don't know why, but I didn't tell anyone at school about Tia. They wouldn't have believed me anyway, or they'd have sent me up for being a snob.

Normally, on my way to and from school, I don't pass Paradise End. I turn left instead of right out of our house and wait at the bottom of the road for one of my friends' mums, who gives us a lift into Torminster on her way to work. But on the second Friday, on my way home, I went the long way round, on a kind of loop, and found myself outside the big gates again.

If you're there, why don't you show yourself? I thought crossly, slowing down and looking in through the bars.

And she did. It was as if she'd heard me. The front door of the great house opened, and she came flying down the long drive, gravel shooting out from under her feet.

She stopped at the gate. She didn't say anything for a moment and I could see she felt embarrassed, as if she was scared she'd looked too keen.

'Hi,' she said at last, blinking nervously. 'I saw you from the window upstairs. Where have you been?'

'Where do you think? At school.'

I must have sounded sharper than I meant to, because her eager smile dropped away.

'Yes, of course. I just meant last weekend.'

'Doing stuff. I've got a lot on.'

'Yes,' she said again. 'Of course.'

I eased my bag off my shoulder and dropped it on the ground. It landed with a clunk.

'Weighs a ton,' I said, flexing my shoulders.

'Have you got mounds of homework then?' She sounded sympathetic.

I shrugged.

'Not that much. I did some in break.'

She was looking sideways and back to me again and I could tell she was just trying to think of something to say.

'Where's your school? Is it near here?' she said at last.

'Not that far. In Torminster. One of my friends' mums gives me a lift in the mornings. I get the bus back. Where's yours?'

'Wiltshire.'

'*Wiltshire?* That's miles away! Must take you all day to get there and back.'

'Only three hours. The traffic's not too bad on Sunday night.'

'You what? You go to school on Sunday?' Something clicked in my mind. 'Oh, I see. It's a boarding school. Must be ripping fun. Midnight feasts and giggles in the dorm.'

I don't know why I was being so horrible and sarcastic. Trying to keep my end up, I suppose.

Tia flushed and bit her lip.

'It's not like that,' she said. 'Not a bit. Anyway, I only board weekly. I'm here at the weekends. And I hate my school. I hate everyone in it.'

'Oh. Sorry.'

I didn't know what else to say. She didn't either. Instead, she pressed the button on the inside of the pillar, and the gates began to swing open.

'Come in,' she said. 'Come up to my bedroom. I've got this . . .'

She stopped, and I could see she was trying to think of something that would tempt me, something she had that I wouldn't be able to resist seeing. She caught my eye and realized I'd sussed her, so she started giggling, and I laughed too and heaved my bag up off the ground.

'OK,' I said. 'Can't stay long though. Mum nearly killed me last time. Lauren kept telling her I'd been done in by a perv.'

'Who's Lauren?' She was leading the way up the drive, past the silver Ferrari I'd seen before, which was pulled up outside one of the garages on the left.

'You don't want to know. My little sister. The world's biggest pain in the bum. Have you got any? Brothers or sisters I mean?'

'A brother.'

'Older or younger?'

'Younger. Much younger.'

We were nearly at the front door. I felt nervous all of a sudden, as if the rest of Tia's family was lying in wait

31

inside, ready to look at me scornfully and tell Tia off for bringing such a scruff to the house.

'My sister drives me crazy,' I said, for something to say. 'She's the worst thing in my life. Doesn't yours, your brother I mean, make you totally mad sometimes?'

'I don't know,' said Tia, taking the big brass ring on the front door and twisting it. 'I've never met him. He lives in Buenos Aires with my father.'

The massive white front door swung open on silent hinges and there I was, following Tia inside.

You know how you make up ideas about places before you go to them? Like when you're on the way to your holiday, and you have a picture in your head of what your room's going to be like in the hotel or the holiday cottage or whatever, and what sort of beach there'll be. And the minute you arrive and see the real thing, the place you'd imagined bursts like a soap bubble, and you can't ever see it in your mind again.

I'd spent years and years imagining the inside of Paradise End, but the real thing was grander, older and much, much more beautiful. More everything, in fact. The main difference, of course, the thing I'd never even thought of, was that there'd be another person, other people, in the house that I'd always dreamed was mine.

We were standing in a great square hall. A wide staircase with delicately carved banisters swept up out of it at the back of the hall to the left, and curved round to become a gallery, that ran above the far end of the hall. There were a couple of enormous rugs on the polished wooden floor, and in the middle stood a table of glowing, polished wood, that was at least four times the size of our kitchen table at home. A bowl of roses, a scarf, a pair of black-leather gloves and a set of keys lay on it. You could have fitted the whole ground floor of our house into that hall easily, with half of moaning Mavis's as well.

I didn't notice everything that first time, like the heavy deep-yellow curtains at the long windows on each side of the front door, or the pictures in curly gold frames that hung on the wood-panelled walls, or the grandfather clock that stood at the bottom of the stairs, marking off the seconds with deep clunking ticks.

Tia was standing still and looking at me. I couldn't think what to say to her, so I went across to the door on the right, which was standing open, and looked into the room.

It was far, far bigger than any sitting room I'd ever been in before, but what I noticed first was the golden colour, the glow on everything, as if the room had caught hold of a sunset and trapped it there. One end was curved, with the three long windows, which I'd so often stared at from the other side of the front gate, set into the bay. More windows ran along the side. Two of them weren't windows at all, but glass doors, and they led out on to the terrace that Tia and I had walked along that first time. There was a huge fireplace at the far end, with a mirror above it that reached right up to the ceiling, and two big blue-and-white China vases on the mantelpiece, with scarlet snakes or dragons or something painted on them. Sofas and armchairs and tables and lamps were dotted around, standing on something pale that looked more like a tapestry than a real carpet. The curtains were thick and

33

heavy, the cushions were fat and soft, the wood was polished and shiny and the paint smelt fresh. It looked like a picture from a magazine.

'This is the drawing room,' said Tia, behind me. She sounded bored. 'I hardly ever come in here. Come and see my room.'

But I was already crossing the hall to the other side, and looking in through the opposite door.

This room was the same shape as the drawing room, with the three windows in the bay at the far end, and four more down the long side. It was a dining room, with a table that stretched forever, a table that you could have seated our whole class at school round, running down the middle of the room, with antique chairs set all round it. The wood shone as brightly as newly fallen chestnuts.

In spite of all the windows, it was darker in here. There was a red-patterned carpet on the floor, and dark-red wallpaper. You hardly noticed the wallpaper, though, because of the big portraits hanging everywhere, all round the room. It was like being in a museum or an art gallery, with people in ancient costumes staring down at you.

'Who's this lot then?' I said, looking round at the pictures. Tia's silence was beginning to rattle me. 'Your uncles and aunties, don't tell me.'

'They're Mimi's,' said Tia. 'Her family.'

'Who's Mimi?'

'Oh, sorry. It's what I call my mother. I used to call her Mummy, but she didn't like it. It made her feel old. She thinks Mimi sounds younger – like a sister. She really wanted me to call her Dixie, like everyone else does, but I wouldn't. Come on, let's go up to my room.'

She seemed to be dying to get out of there, and kept looking at me nervously, as if she was scared that all this grandeur would put me off her. Actually, her nervousness was making me feel better because I'd started to get edgy. It was all too much. Too strange. Totally over the top.

I pointed to the biggest picture. It was of a guy in a black suit, looking pleased with himself. I guessed he was a Victorian. The artist had painted a window beside him and outside it you could see an old-fashioned town with factory chimneys rising up out of it. He'd even painted in the smoke.

'That was Mimi's great-grandfather,' Tia said. 'He bought this house. He lived here.'

'Can't have done.' I wasn't really thinking about what I was saying. I just wanted to keep my end up, I suppose. 'A mad old miser used to live here. Everyone knows that. He wandered around in the buff with his willy hanging out.'

'Oh, there you are, darling,' said a voice from the door. 'And who on earth is this?'

My heart jumped so high it practically shot up into my mouth. I was prickling all over with embarrassment. It had been so quiet I hadn't even thought that anyone else could be in the house. I'd assumed we were on our own.

A woman was standing in the doorway. The first thing I noticed was the waft of perfume drifting out from her like an invisible cloud. Then I saw that she was tall and amazingly slim, and that her hair, pale and silky, fell in a soft sheet to her shoulders. I can't remember what she was wearing – clinging blue trousers, I think, and a top that shone as she moved. I thought she was the most beautiful person I'd ever seen, like someone from a magazine, but fragile too, as if a gust of wind could have bent her over.

She was looking at me. Her eyes were the same sea colour as Tia's. I stared back. My mouth was hanging open, I expect, in an embarrassing way, but I was noticing something strange, a kind of blurring round her eyes and an uncertain, drooping twist to her mouth. If she'd been a painting, instead of a living person, you'd have thought the artist's brush had wobbled.

Beside me, I felt Tia stiffen.

'This is Carly, Mimi,' she said quickly. 'She's a friend of Camilla's. She lives just near here. We've played tennis together at Camilla's house.'

I nearly turned my head to stare disbelievingly at Tia, but I stopped myself in time. She was giving me an alibi, I could see that. I could just imagine what would have happened if she'd said, 'This is Carly, she lives in that three-bedroom semi down the street, the one with the paint chipped off the front door, she's got a revolting little sister called Lauren, she goes to that rough comprehensive on the edge of Torminster, I've got no idea who she is, I just picked her up outside our front gates, and by the way we've decided to be friends.'

It would have been, 'Out you go, you dirty common little girl. This is no place for the likes of you.'

At least, that's what I thought Tia's mum would have said.

Instead, she looked at me vaguely and said, 'Near here? Good heavens. I didn't think anyone lived in this wilderness.' Her voice was odd, a little thick and slow. 'Camilla's mother is amazing. She knows simply everyone.' She flashed me a smile that was so lovely I almost gasped, but shut it off her face at once, as if to tell me that she hadn't meant it. Then she turned back to Tia.

'You'll have to have supper on you own tonight after all, darling. Lally rang. She's having a party, and Max Starsky's going to be there. He's over here from LA. What a lucky chance! Otto's taking me up in his car. Graziella will do you something on a tray.'

'Mimi!' Tia's voice was sharp with disappointment. 'You said you'd be at home tonight. You promised! Who's Max Starsky anyway?'

Her mother gave a trilling laugh.

'Only the *hottest* new director in Hollywood. As if you didn't know!' She had already turned away. 'Now don't be a bore, sweetie. I've absolutely promised Lally. Get your little friend to stay. Carly, is it? I'm sure you'll have lots of fun, both of you.'

She turned, putting a hand on the door frame to steady herself, and went out, and the room seemed suddenly darker.

I turned to look at Tia. She was biting her lip.

'Every Friday.' He voice was shaky, and I couldn't decide if she was angry or trying not to cry. 'She does this to me every single Friday. I thought at least this weekend, when I'd got a half-day and was home so early . . .'

She stopped. I nearly asked her something about Camilla, whoever she was, but I didn't. Camilla had been my entry ticket, that was all. Somehow, I didn't like to ask her about Otto, whoever he was, either.

'I thought I was going to die of embarrassment just then,' I said, trying to cheer Tia up. 'Do you think she

37

heard me say all that stuff about the mad miser and his willy?'

Tia's face lightened. She grabbed my arm and pulled me towards the door. I was glad to get out of that gloomy old dining room anyway. The pictures were giving me the creeps, especially the one of the old guy, with all his smoky factories.

'Who cares?' she said. 'He was a miser, as a matter of fact, old Joshua Braithwaite. And it's true, he did go a bit mad in the end. Quite dotty really. I didn't know he showed people his thing though. How thrilling. Wish I'd seen it.'

'But he was your great-great-something-grandfather,' I said, slightly shocked.

'So what?' A change had come over Tia. She seemed happier and more carefree all of a sudden, as if a worry had gone. 'Everyone's got weird ancestors. I bet you have.'

'I haven't got any ancestors,' I said. 'Well, not that I know about. Except for Mum's great-uncle Albert. He was killed in the First World War. He got shell shock and jumped out of his trench one night, shouting rude words at the Germans. They shot him.'

'There, you see?' said Tia. 'You've only got one ancestor, and he wasn't exactly ordinary either.'

'My nan's OK though.' We were walking up the great staircase and I was running my hand up the banister, loving the touch of the wood, as smooth as silk. 'There's nothing wrong with her, I can tell you. She practically runs the community centre down in Hartwell-on-Sea, and the only time she goes mad is when kids break in and smash the place up.'

We'd got to the top of the staircase now and were standing on the gallery there, looking down into the hall below.

'This is so amazing,' I said, letting myself sound impressed for once. 'I can't believe I'm here.'

'You wouldn't, would you,' Tia said suddenly, 'stay, I mean? For supper? Graziella's a brilliant cook.'

'I can't. I told you. Mum'll do her nut if I'm not home soon. She's probably rung round the undertakers already.'

'Call her then,' said Tia. 'My mobile's in my bedroom. Tell her you're here and that you'll be late home.'

'I don't know,' I said, but I did. I knew I wanted to stay, and that I'd make Mum let me, however much she moaned about it.

5

I don't know what I'd expected Tia's bedroom to be like, that first time, but when I stepped into it, before I'd looked round properly, I thought it was like a dream of everything everyone thinks they want. And come to think of it, of everything they didn't even know they wanted in the first place.

The room was big for one thing. Big? Enormous, just like the rooms downstairs. There were three long windows along one wall, and two along another wall, and the sun was streaming in, making everything dazzle.

The bed was double, a four poster, with white-muslin curtains and cushions and soft toys piled up on it, and there was a rose-coloured sofa and a couple of pink armchairs, and a white desk, miles long, with a computer on it, and bookshelves full of new books, and pictures of horses and women in white dresses in frames on the walls.

'Do you like it?' Tia said. 'I don't. I wanted it to be purple and silver. But Mimi thinks I'm still four years old and she made the designer do everything in pink.'

'The designer?' My mouth fell open. 'You mean someone else designed all this? Didn't you choose your stuff yourself?'

Tia shook her head.

'No. I wanted to, but I don't suppose I'd have been any good at it. Mimi says I'd have only made it look a mess, but I think it looks a mess now.'

I saw what she meant. The candy pink of the armchairs, the pink roses on the curtains and the pictures on the walls were sickly and babyish now that I looked more closely.

'I bet you'd have done it better,' I said. 'At least you wouldn't have done everything in pink. This lot looks like a pile of candyfloss with jelly beans stuck all over it.'

I must have sounded nastier than I meant to, because she bit her lip and looked hurt. I should have said something nice to take the sting away, but I was too busy looking round the room, feeling jealous and irritated that Tia had so much and she'd done so little with it. I was doing a light-ning plan in my head of what I'd do if the room was mine.

'You could add some purple stuff anyway,' I said. 'It would go with the pink. You could dye your bedspread purple. And those cushion covers.'

'Dye the bedspread?' She was staring at me. 'Can you get things dyed? I didn't know.'

'You don't get things dyed. You do it yourself,' I said impatiently. 'You get a tin of dye, read the instructions, shove it all in the washing machine, and there you are! Mum's always dyeing stuff round our house when things get stained and faded and all that. It's fun.'

'Wow.' Tia looked scared and excited at the same time. 'I couldn't though. I couldn't possibly.'

'Why not?'

'Mimi would kill me. This bedspread comes from Switzerland. It's handmade Thai silk.'

'It wouldn't spoil it or anything,' I said, though I was beginning to feel doubtful. 'At least, I don't think it would. It would just change the colour. Know what I'd do? I'd dye it first and have the row afterwards.'

She wrinkled her nose.

'How would I get the dye?'

I sighed impatiently.

'You'd go out of the house and down the lane,' I said, as if I was talking to a small child, 'and catch the bus to Torminster. Then you'd go to Hardwicke's in the high street, and . . .'

'I've never been on a bus. I wouldn't know what to do.'

'You've never been on a . . . Oh.'

That shut me up. I couldn't have been more amazed if she'd said she'd never eaten a pizza or been to the cinema. The funny thing was that I didn't envy her this grand, big bedroom any more. It felt like a hotel room, a place that wasn't hers at all.

'What's your room like?' she asked.

I took a deep breath. I didn't know where to begin. You couldn't imagine anything more different than Tia's room and our bedroom at home.

'Well,' I said feebly. 'I don't know how to describe it really.'

And I didn't. Not to Tia anyway. For a start I couldn't bear to tell her that I had to share it with my horrible little sister, and that it was so small it would have fitted into hers about five times over.

As a matter of fact, between you and me, I don't think I've done too badly, given what I've had to start from. I've got these tap-dance posters – you should see them – all over my side of the room. They're in black and white, and really cool. They gave me the idea to make black and white a theme, to create a sort of style. Don't get the wrong idea. 'Style' sounds much too grand. I mean, I haven't got much space, and all the furniture's been there forever and looks as if it came out of a junk shop, and I can't do anything about the yellow walls, so I have to try and imagine the look I want.

The posters are the main thing, and I've stuck an old white beaded shawl that my nan gave me on the wall above my bed and draped a black scarf round the lamp-shade. The light effect's good. Kind of weird, but good. Our clothes are on a rail behind a curtain. Hardly room for anything, of course, and Lauren takes more than half the hangers, but I've got my own shelf under my own mirror for my make-up, and my own desk. OK, so it's more a shelf than a desk, but I keep my school stuff on it, and my mascot (he's a little green monster and I know he's embarrassing, but I've had him since I was a baby and I really love him), and this stunning black vase that I got in the school garage sale, to keep my pencils in.

Stand on Lauren's side and turn your back on all her junky little kid's stuff and look at my half of the room with your eyes nearly closed, and it's not that bad really, when I've tidied it up. Only usually everything's buried under mounds of clothes.

'Anyway,' I said, taking a deep breath, as I tried to think how to explain all this to Tia. 'I've got these fantastic posters. They're all on tap dance.' I could see a puzzled crease between her eyes, but I'd got going now so I went on. 'My first was a big one of Fred Astaire and Ginger Rogers. It's so classy, you've no idea. And then I wrote off for my Savion Glover. That's brilliant. And I've got the Tap Dogs now too. They're amazing. All boots and Levi's. Really powerful.'

I stopped. Tia's eyebrows were raised in questioning points above her eyes. She didn't have the faintest idea what I was talking about, I could tell. I gave up.

You'd probably think they were boring if you ever got to see them, I said silently in my head, and the contrast between my horrible, cramped, shared bedroom and Tia's luxury palace hit me all over again.

'It's all a mess at home,' I said out loud.

She looked as if she was about to ask a whole stack of questions, so to get her off the subject I said quickly, 'Where do you keep your clothes? There aren't any cupboards in here.'

'They're in my dressing room,' said Tia.

'Your what?'

I couldn't help the way it came out, with a snort. 'My dressing room'. I mean.

She opened one of a pair of doors at the far end of her bedroom. I followed her, and looked over her shoulder into a much smaller room (well, it was still bigger than Sam's room at home), with cupboards all the way down one side, and a dressing-table thing with mirrors on it at one end.

Then she opened one of the cupboard doors, and pure envy attacked me again, biting me like a little green snake sliding out from nowhere and shooting a dose of poison into my veins.

I just stood there, looking at Tia's clothes. There were hundreds of them. Thousands of them! Jackets and tops, trousers, skirts, hats – hats! – and whole racks of party stuff, velvet and chiffon and Lycra and satin, beads and feathers and bits of sparkle. And shoes! Leather boots (pairs and pairs of them) and strappy sandals and silvery slipper things, and shoes for doing special things in, like riding boots, and rope soles for the beach, and those green-soled shoes for tennis. No tap shoes though, or ballet. I was glad about that, in a way.

'Shame, isn't it,' I said nastily, 'that you can only ever wear one pair of shoes at a time?'

I'm not sure if she heard me. She'd opened a door off her dressing room into a bathroom.

I knew what to expect by now. It would be the glitziest bathroom I'd ever seen, all sparkly and tiled with gold bits everywhere. I was right. It was.

'Aren't you the lucky one,' I said. 'Sell these gold taps and you could feed an African family for a year.'

That's the sort of thing Mum says sometimes, and it always infuriates me. I couldn't believe I'd said it myself.

'I know.' She looked embarrassed. 'Don't think I wanted all this stuff. I didn't.'

'Don't tell me. It was done by designers.'

'Yes. Mimi just told them to do the most expensive thing they could because Daddy was paying for it. She didn't care what it looked like as long as it cost him as much as possible.'

'Why?'

'I don't know. It's the way she feels about him, I suppose. She really hates him now.'

I shivered. It was as if I'd smelt something nasty. The glitzy bathroom was giving me the creeps.

'At least you've got it to yourself,' I said, trying to think of something nice to say. 'In our house you've only been in the bathroom for a nanosecond when everyone's banging on the door telling you to get the hell out of there.'

She pounced on this. I couldn't believe how fascinated she was by my boringly ordinary life.

'How many people are there then, in your family? Do you live with both your parents? Are they together?'

'Yes. And there's Lauren and Sam. I told you about Lauren. Sam's my older brother.'

'You are lucky,' she said again, and I was amazed to see that she looked as jealous of me as I'd been feeling of her a few minutes earlier. 'I always wanted an older brother. It must be fantastic.'

I stared at her.

'Tia, Sam's the biggest pain in the butt you ever met. Think lazy slob crossed with flashes of Rottweiler and the biggest ego in Northern Europe. Except when he wants to borrow my Walkman, which he does all the time, since his was bust. Then smarmy's not the word for it. I'm telling you, a brother like Sam is a living, breathing assault on my human rights.'

'Oh.' She looked disappointed. 'But don't you do things together? Go to films, or go out for meals or something?'

'Me?' I burst out laughing. 'Go out with Sam? You seriously have to be kidding. I mean kidding.'

'Some people go round with their brothers.' Tia sounded almost obstinate. 'Mimi used to go to dances with Frost whenever they weren't quarrelling.'

'Frost?'

I was staring at her, mystified. Visions of her mum wrapped up in winter woollies dancing through the snow flashed through my head.

She smiled at the look on my face.

'Frost's my uncle,' she said. 'He's Mimi's twin brother.'

'Right.' I sat down on the sofa beside her. 'Let's get this straight. You've got an uncle whose name is Frost?'

Tia threw her head back and laughed.

'I wish you could see your face, Carly. Frost's only his nickname. His real name's Frederick, but no one ever calls him that.'

'I don't blame them.' I shook my head. 'You could call him Fred though. Why Frost?'

Before she could answer, somewhere in that huge house, miles away, a telephone rang. I clapped my hand over my mouth.

'Mum! I haven't called her!'

Tia jumped up, grabbed a slim mobile in a mint-green cover from beside her bed and put it into my hands.

I dialled the number, and as it rang I turned away. I didn't want Tia to hear the racket there always was in our house at five o'clock in the afternoon – Sam yelling about his lost football boots, and Lauren with the TV turned up to maximum, and Mum screeching at her to turn it down.

Mum answered it herself, thank goodness.

'Carly? Are you all right? Where are you? Did they keep you in after school? They should have let me know.'

'No, Mum. I'm at Tia's. At Paradise End. She says I can stay to tea.'

'Oh.' Mum sounded doubtful. 'I don't know. What about your homework?'

'Done most of it. Please, Mum.'

'Look, Carly.' She was thinking of reasons to say no. I could almost hear them clicking round in her brain. 'I've got the tea half ready now. You could have given me a bit of notice. Anyway, they won't have catered for you. You can't just land on people like that.'

'It's not like that here, Mum. It's OK. Really.'

'No, love.' She was firming herself up, I could tell. 'We're doing your costume for the display tonight. I want you back here by six. We can fix another time for you to stay longer when I've had a word with Tia's mother. Is she there now? Can I speak to her?'

The thought of my mum talking to Tia's 'Mimi' made my skin prickle all over with embarrassment.

'No! She's out. Tia's on her own. That's why she wants me to stay.'

'I see.' Mum's voice was even more disapproving, and I knew I'd lost. Mum's so weird about me being in my friends' houses if no one else is in. I don't know what she thinks we're going to do. Set fire to the place? Bomb our skulls out on drugs? Invite loads of sex-crazed boys round and have an orgy? I know this boring old village keeps growing (it'll be a town soon, at this rate), but it's not exactly the vice capital of the Western world. Too much imagination, that's Mum's trouble.

'Back at six,' she was saying firmly. 'You can bring Tia round here if you like, but I want you home. Lauren! For God's sake turn that thing down! You'll have Mavis pounding on the wall in a minute.'

I switched off the little green phone and handed it back to Tia.

'This thing's so cool,' I said. 'Where did you get it?'

'New York,' said Tia, making me gulp. 'What did your mother say?'

'She won't let me stay. I didn't think she would, actually. She's dead strict about me being with people she doesn't know. Worse than Dad, even though he's a . . .'

I stopped.

Trust my big mouth, I was thinking. If you want to turn her off right away, try telling her your dad's a policeman.

'He's a what?' Tia was leaning forwards.

'Nothing.'

'No, you were going to say. What is he then, your father? What does he do?'

At that moment, her posh accent really got to me. It really riled me. I stood up.

'He's in the police force,' I said. 'Look, I've got to go.'

But Tia was looking up at me, fascinated.

'Wow! But isn't it dangerous? Don't you get scared in case he gets hurt?'

No one had ever said that to me before. It had always been things like, 'Must be wicked doing those high-speed chases,' or 'Better not tell my brother. He hates the pigs,' or 'Watch out, here comes Sergeant Carly.'

I sat down again.

'Mum gets worried when he's out late at the weekend, sorting out drunks and fights and stuff when that big pub on the Crossways roundabout closes. He nearly got his face cut up with a Stanley knife last weekend.'

'That's just so scary,' said Tia, shuddering.

49

She was seriously impressed, I could tell. I leaned back against the silky rose-coloured sofa cushions, ready to show off. I try to keep as quiet as possible about Dad at school, but it was different with Tia. She wasn't part of my world. She didn't know anyone in it. She was looking in on us from the outside.

'He was doing a drugs bust last week,' I began. 'Out on the bypass. Heroin dealers. They were squatting in an empty farmhouse. Dad and his team surrounded the place, wearing flak jackets and all, and . . .'

Her little green mobile bleeped out strange chiming noises, not like anything I'd heard before, really unusual and classy.

It was just as well, I suppose. My imagination was beginning to take over. Dad's drug bust (actually, he'd only mentioned weed, not crack or heroin or anything) was getting mixed up with something I'd seen on TV.

Tia had the phone to her ear now. She flicked her long blonde hair back and looked at me apologetically.

'Hiya, Frost. No, Mimi's out. Yes, with Otto. They've gone to Lally's. There's a director Mimi wants to meet or something. I'm all right, really. No, I'm not on my own. I've got a friend here. Carly. What? No, she's staying all evening. Please, Frost. Don't fuss. Mimi won't be back late. She promised. Yes, of course Graziella's here. I'm fine, really. Bye.'

'But I can't stay,' I said as she snapped the little phone shut. 'Mum said I've got to be back by six, and it's nearly that now.'

'I know. Sorry. I just didn't want him to make a scene.

50

He'll be furious with Mimi for going out this evening. They'll have a row about it. They've been awful recently, since Mimi started going round with Otto. They fight all the time.'

'What about?' I wanted to keep her mind off Dad and my silly drugs story. Anyway, Tia's family sounded so weird and interesting I wanted to know all about them.

'Otto usually.' She screwed her face up as she said his name. 'And me sometimes. Frost keeps telling Mimi she's a useless mother. He's no good with people himself though, so I don't blame her for getting furious when he ticks her off.'

I didn't say anything. I wanted her to go on.

'And they're always fighting over the house.'

'What? Paradise End?'

'Yes. My grandfather left it to both of them when he died, but Mimi was away acting all the time. And when—'

'Wait. Stop!' I interrupted. 'What do you mean, she was away acting?'

'She's an actress. Didn't I say?'

'No.' I was tingling with excitement. 'Is she famous? Do I know her? Have I seen her in anything?'

Tia shrugged.

'You might have. She had a brilliant part about fifteen years ago. She was Claudia in *Girl on a Beach*.'

I shook my head reluctantly. I'd never heard of *Girl on a Beach*.

'Is it on DVD? I'd love to see it.'

She looked away.

'Yes, I've got it. I could lend it to you.'

51

'What else? Has she been on TV? In soaps or anything?'

'No. Just a few things. Nothing much.'

Her voice was colourless. She stood up and went across to the window, standing with her back to me, looking out. Even I, with my thick elephant hide, could tell that somehow I'd offended her. I was burning with more questions, but I bit my lip and shut up.

After a moment, she said, without turning round, 'I was born after *Girl on a Beach*, just when she was making her breakthrough. She had loads of wonderful offers, but she couldn't take any of them up because of me.'

As plain as could be, I could hear Mum's voice in my head.

Never blame other people for things you fail to do yourself.

'That's got to be rubbish,' I said. 'If she was really good, having a baby wouldn't have stopped her.'

'But it did. Her face went puffy and she got fat, she says. She lost her looks.'

'What do you mean? She's the most beautiful person I've ever seen in my life. Who says she lost her looks?'

'She does. It's what she thinks anyway. She's told me so hundreds of times.'

She'd turned her back to me again and I couldn't see her face. I felt my fingers curl up into fists.

'Tia, that's just cruel and stupid,' I burst out. 'Having a baby never stopped Madonna or – or Demi Moore or Catherine Zeta Jones or anyone. There had to be other reasons. Showbiz is a tough old world. You have to take the rough with the smooth.'

I could hear Mrs Litvinov speaking through me, and I

52

was afraid for a moment that I'd sounded silly, but when she turned to me, and I saw a smile flit across her face, I knew I'd said the right thing.

'Oh, I can't really see Mimi taking the rough,' she said. 'She can hardly cope with the tiny little bumps in the smooth. She gets furious if things even get a bit wobbly.'

'There you are then.' I was triumphant. 'She probably got all proud and conceited after her first big role, thought she was the world's biggest star and started putting people down and making herself really unpopular. Teamwork in performance is so . . .'

But I could see from her face that she'd had enough snippets of Carly wisdom for one day. Then I remembered something.

'Hang on a minute. I thought you said she was never here because she was acting all the time. How come she's away so much if she never gets any more roles?'

'Oh, she does sometimes. Only little ones though. But mostly she's seeing agents and going to parties where there are directors and people. That's how she met Otto. He's an actor, only he hasn't had any breaks yet. Mimi's totally potty about him. She keeps taking him round to meet everyone. She says he's going to make it big, and then because he's her partner he'll make sure she gets the parts she deserves. But he's just using her, I know he is. He'll climb up her like a ladder, then kick her over when he reaches the top of the wall.'

There was a hard note in Tia's voice that I hadn't heard before.

'You really hate him, don't you?'

She made a face.

'He's not worth hating. I just don't like it when – well, when Mimi goes crazy about people who don't care about her at all, and she goes silly and can't think about anything else and . . .'

Otto's not the first one then, I thought.

The new me, the sensitive Carly, knew it was time to back off.

'Go on about Frost then,' I said, trying not to smile at his name.

'What about him?'

'How come they're living together, Frost and your mum? I couldn't ever live with Sam, not once we're grown up.'

'Oh, that.' She shook her hair back, as if she was bored with the subject. 'When my parents divorced and Mimi decided we'd live at Paradise End, my father said that as part of the divorce settlement he'd pay to do it up. Frost was jealous or something, I think, and he said if she was going to live here, he would too, and they're sharing it now. Mimi lives here all the time, and Frost stays when he's in Britain, except that he's usually in Zurich, where he does something in a bank. I don't know why Mimi decided to live here. She hates not being in town. She'd much rather live in New York or Paris or the middle of London. Sometimes I think she only stays here because she can't bear the thought of Frost having it all to himself. Look, all this is so boring. You can't possibly want to hear all about my ghastly family.'

'Yes, I do.' I was totally riveted. I'd never heard anything like it. There'd never been anything so interesting and sneaky in my family. Mum and her sisters argue sometimes, and Dad complains that his brother never writes or phones except at Christmas, though Birmingham isn't exactly a million miles away, but that's about it. Tia's family sounded as if it had walked straight out of an over-the-top American soap. 'Go on,' I said. 'Tell me more. Who's Otto? What's he like really? He can't be all bad. He must be a bit nice.'

Then, as I looked at her, her face seemed to close up. She clenched her fists fiercely and said something really strange.

'I'm waiting, that's what I'm doing. I'm spending my whole life waiting, keeping quiet, out of harm's way. I know it sounds weird, but that's what it feels like. I'm just waiting to be free of them all, to find out . . .'

'Find out what, Tia?'

'What sort of person I really am.'

She sounded almost angry. I wanted her to go on, but she wouldn't. If I'd been feeling prickly, I'd have thought she was being stand-offish or snobbish, but I knew it wasn't that. It was as if she'd panicked all of a sudden. For some reason or other, she was scared of saying too much, of letting me see too much.

I went home then, and I knew, as the gates of Paradise End swung shut behind me, with Tia on the other side of them, that in spite of all her stunning clothes, and her gold taps, and her pink-silk sofa, and her hand-made-Thai-silk bedspread, I didn't really need to envy her.

I looked back, when I was halfway down the short distance of street that separated her huge metal gates from our broken wooden one. She was waving at me, her arm stretched out through the bars, almost as if she was a prisoner, signalling to someone in the free world outside.

6

It was tap the next day, of course, being Saturday. In the warm-up practice session, Mrs Litvinov put me with Lizzie Fraser, who was going to do the hip-hop number with Simone in the display. I'm quite good friends with Lizzie. She doesn't go to my school, so we don't go round together with the same crowd, but that's fine by me. My tap's my own, and I keep it separate from school. I don't mind sharing it a bit with Lizzie, who's quite good (though not as good as me, to be honest), but I don't want anyone else in on it, thank you very much.

That's a thing I've discovered about life. It's good to keep things separate. I don't like mixing school and home (except for a few best friends, the ones I can really trust), and I don't like muddling up tap with school. Now I was finding out that I didn't want to mix Tia and Paradise End with any of the other bits of my life. They were in a special compartment, on their own.

Tap was tough that day. I don't know what had got into Mrs Litvinov.

'Rhythm! Keep in time with the music!' she barked at us. 'Stop dreaming, Carly. What's the matter with you? Think that's dancing? Looks more like the mad

57

tramplings of a wounded elephant. Now pull yourself together and tap!'

She'd never spoken to me like that before. I had to blink tears out of my eyes. Lizzie was lovely about it. She said, out of the corner of her mouth, 'Silly old bat. She'll look like an elephant herself soon if she gets any fatter.'

Lizzie was really unlucky, though, because Mrs Litvinov heard, and she turned on Lizzie and tore her off the biggest strip ever, so that Lizzie was the one who was nearly crying, and all I could do was give her sympathetic looks and mouth 'Sorry' at her.

Things were better after that, thank God, because the music started getting to me, the way it always does, and the rhythm kicked in, and there was that sudden magical click that judders through me, and my heart lifts, and my scalp tingles, and my feet start to go, and nothing can get in the way then. Nothing can go wrong.

It wasn't good enough for Mrs Litvinov though. She called Lizzie and me over when the music stopped.

'It's all very well getting carried away.' She was frowning at us in that really scary way she has, when her nose starts to look pinched, and her hair, which is very curly, seems to go hard, bouncing round her head like black-metal bedsprings. 'You can't count on inspiration to carry you through when you're up there on the stage dancing in front of Mr and Mrs General Public. Stage fright and inspiration don't always go together, and then you'll need technique to carry you through. And your toe hops, Carly, are a total disgrace. Turn your feet out on the day like that, and you'll trip yourself up, never mind Lizzie. You do it like this. Look.'

And off she went into a perfect routine.

'Now, Lizzie, as for you . . .'

She started on a whole thing about Lizzie's springs, and I stopped listening, because I'd seen Lauren out of the corner of my eye, standing at the door with a grin all over her weaselly little face, and I could tell she was just loving it, hearing us being ticked off.

'Costumes,' said Mrs Litvinov, finishing with Lizzie at last. 'How are they coming along?'

'We're working on it, me and Mum,' I said quickly, with a sideways look at Lizzie. 'Mum's going to get in touch with you this week.'

The truth was that nothing had happened. Mum kept saying she was about to start, but she never seemed to get round to it. Last night had been typical. She'd dragged me back from Tia's to work on it, and then the phone hadn't stopped ringing, and every time we'd got going, Lauren had interfered, and then Mum and I had had a row because her ideas were so horribly, awfully, cheapskate and sad, and then I'd gone to bed in what was, quite frankly, a filthy mood.

'Mrs Litvinov's right about technique, isn't she?' Lauren said as we pushed open the swing doors of the Wellesley Centre and walked out into the busy Saturday-morning high street. 'Miss Tideswell says I'm—'

'One more word,' I said, stopping dead, grabbing her by the arm and wagging my finger in her face, 'one word, and I'll . . .'

I stopped. I couldn't think of anything bad enough to threaten her with.

'You'll what?' said Lauren, looking pleased and excited,

the way she does when she manages to get me to lose my temper.

Maybe it was because we were on our own, without Mum and Dad being there, or perhaps it was just that it was so easy to read her poor little mind. Whatever. Instead of losing my cool I started to laugh.

'One day,' I said, 'you'll go too far, and your body'll be found cut up in little chunks in dustbin bags on the rubbish dump.'

She looked a bit disappointed.

'No, but what are you going to do to me, if I don't shut up? You haven't said.'

'I'm going to buy a packet of Starburst and not give you any.' And I grabbed her hand and plunged across the road towards the newsagent on the other side.

'Do you think, Carly,' Lauren said, as we came out of the newsagent and walked along towards the bus stop, 'that if I work really, really hard . . .' – she made a sort of gloopy noise as she moved her Starburst from one cheek to the other – 'that I'll ever be as good at tap as you are?'

I looked at her suspiciously.

'You can't have another yet. You haven't finished the first.'

'No, I mean it.' She was looking at me quite seriously. 'Miss Tideswell says you're the best they've had at the Wellesley Centre for years and years. Do you think it runs in the family? Do you, Carly?'

'Search me,' I said, and it was just as well that the bus came along at that moment, and that we had to run for it, because I might have handed the whole packet to her and regretted it for the rest of the day.

*

We were just finishing off clearing up after lunch (Mum does a proper one on Saturdays, with sausages or spag bol or something) when the phone rang. Mum picked it up, but I was standing so close to her that I could hear every word of the voice at the other end. It was a woman, and she was speaking in a loud, posh voice. I could even hear her heavy, unsteady breathing.

'Mrs McQuarrie?'

'Yes?' Mum said guardedly. I knew she was thinking it might be someone making trouble for Dad, and was ready to hang up.

'I gather you're a friend of Margaret Marchmont, Camilla's mother,' the disembodied voice went on, and my blood started freezing in my veins.

I could see that Mum was just about to say, 'Sorry, I think you've got the wrong person,' and put the phone down, so I hissed at her, 'Don't! It's Tia's mother.'

'Oh,' Mum said, looking at me, and I could see she was so surprised that the stuff about Camilla and her mother hadn't sunk in.

I was straining to hear, flapping my hands at Sam, who'd come back into the kitchen to look for his jacket.

'This is Dixie Braithwaite,' Tia's mother was saying. 'Your little girl, Carly, seems to have chummed up rather with Tia, my daughter. Awfully nice for them both to find a kindred spirit in this neck of the woods, don't you think?'

She gave a loud, unnecessary laugh, and Mum held the phone away from her ear. Sam started whistling, I glared at him, he put up his hands as if pretending to fend me off, saw his jacket where he'd dumped it on the washing

61

machine, picked it up and went out of the back door, banging it shut behind him.

'Er, yes,' Mum said, making one of her God-this-is-weird-I-don't-get-it-at-all faces.

'Would you mind frightfully if Carly came over this afternoon?' Tia's mother went on. 'Unfortunately I have to dash out, and Tia's rather at a loose end. Weekends do stretch on, don't they?'

'Well . . .' said Mum, and I held my breath. She was always moaning on about weekends passing quicker than a snowstorm in summer, what with the washing and the shopping and the housework and her heaps and heaps of marking, and I was dead scared she'd start saying as much.

There was a pause and I heard a clinking sound at the other end.

'Do you want me to send someone over to pick Carly up?' Tia's mother went on, 'Or can she manage to get here under her own steam?'

'What? Good grief, she can walk,' said Mum sharply. 'It's only two minutes up the road.'

'Oh.' Tia's mother sounded surprised. I imagined her mentally scanning the streets round Paradise End, thinking she must have missed something. 'How marvellous. Tia will be thrilled.'

'What time do you want Carly to come up then?' Mum was never much of a one for speeches, but she sounded even more abrupt than usual, and I knew she was thinking that Tia's mother was talking a load of gush.

'The sooner the better!' Tia's mother said with a another laugh. 'You know what girls are like. Friendship is all at that age, isn't it?'

No one knows more about girls of my age than Mum. She teaches classrooms full every day. I crossed my fingers behind my back, hoping she wasn't going to start.

'Did you say you were going out yourself?' she said, frowning at the telephone.

'Oh, you mustn't worry about that.' Tia's mother laughed again. 'The housekeeper will be here. Graziella's a great friend of Tia's. Awfully good with her. She'll keep an eye on things and do them some supper. Such a bore that I can't be here myself, but duty calls, I'm afraid.'

'It's very kind of you, Mrs um . . .' said Mum, turning to look at me and raising her eyebrows. I nodded my head so hard that my teeth started rattling. 'Carly would love to come. I'd like her back here at a reasonable time though. She has her homework to do.'

'Of course.' I could hear her relief buzzing down the wire. 'Tia will be thrilled. So lovely to talk to you. We must get together for lunch one day.'

Mum opened her mouth, about to protest, but the phone had already gone down at the other end.

'Lunch, eh?' she said, turning to me, and I could see that a smile was puckering up her red cheeks. 'I think I can see it, can't you? "Sorry, Class 7B. Can't take you for geography today. I'm going out to lunch with –" What did you say her name was?'

'Dixie. Dixie Braithwaite.'

A little crease appeared in Mum's forehead.

'Where have I heard that name before?'

'No idea,' I said quickly. I didn't want Mum to remember about Dixie being an actress. She might have heard all sorts of awful things about her. 'Tia's not like her mum

63

anyway. Not one little bit. She's really nice. Anyway, she's lonely. She's only here at the weekends, because she goes to boarding school, and her mother went out last night too. Tia was dead upset about it. She needs company.'

'I see,' said Mum sarcastically. 'Babysitting – is that what they want you for?' She must have seen the fury in my face, because she threw up her hands in surrender. 'Sorry, love. That was unfair. I suppose it can't be much fun for her, rattling around on her own in that great big barn of a place. All right, Carly. Off you go. As a matter of fact I haven't got a spare second this afternoon to do your costume, what with the ironing and all.'

She looked so harassed that I felt almost guilty.

'I'll give you a hand tomorrow, Mum, honestly I will,' I said, and I gave her a hug and kiss on her damp cheek, and dashed upstairs to find something that I could wear, which might, with a huge stretch of the imagination, have just possibly come out of Tia's amazing wardrobe.

7

'How did you get my phone number?' I asked Tia as we walked up the gravel drive together towards the house. She'd been waiting inside the gate when I arrived, pretending to practise her tennis strokes. 'I didn't give it to you, did I? And we're not in the book. Dad had to go ex-directory after we had some nasty calls from a con.'

'It took a bit of a hunt.' Tia looked pleased with herself. 'I like doing that kind of thing. It makes me feel I'm beating the system. It wasn't terribly difficult anyway. I remembered the directories in the library. The local one's years out of date, but I thought you just might be in it, and there you were.'

'In the library?' I was surprised. 'I didn't know they kept phone books there. I thought they only had fiction and history and videos and stuff.'

Tia looked a bit self-conscious.

'Not the public library. Our library. Didn't you see it the other day? Come on. I'll show it to you now.'

'No,' I said quickly. 'Let's go up to your room.'

I didn't want to see another grand room in Paradise End just yet. The gold drawing room and the red dining room had made me feel about ten centimetres tall. I wanted to leave the library for another day.

'OK,' said Tia. She didn't seem to mind.

I followed her up the stairs. It was only the second time I'd walked up those wide, shallow steps, letting my hand linger on the smooth banister rail as I'd done before, while I looked up at the old pictures in their curvy frames, but already I felt I was beginning to know it. I could cope with the hall and the stairs. I'd taken possession of them in a new kind of way in my mind.

A bit at a time, I told myself. I can handle this a bit at a time. And inside me there was a spark of pride and a voice saying, Look at me, walking up these stairs as if they really did belong to me.

At the top I stopped, and looked down over the gallery rail into the hall below. Light was flooding into it through the long front windows, streaming across the floor from the open door of the drawing room, that was filled with golden sunshine. The brilliance of it made the reds and blues of the rugs glow, lustrous and warm. I took a deep breath and smelt furniture polish and roses. The clock at the foot of the stairs ticked peacefully, loud and unhurried. It was the only sound.

I could feel the beauty of Paradise End wrapping its tendrils round me again, drawing me in. I pushed the horrible things out of my mind – Tia's loneliness, her lack of freedom, her strange, unhappy family. I just wanted to be there, in that lovely house, to pretend to myself that I belonged in it.

A horrible small voice inside my head said, You only

want to be Tia's friend because you like coming here. You're using her.

At that moment, I reckon it was telling the truth.

Then, from behind a closed door downstairs, someone turned on a radio. I looked at Tia. She'd been leaning over the gallery rail beside me, as if she understood my mood.

'I thought your mum had gone out,' I said.

She bent down to brush something off her shoe, and her hair flopped over her face.

'She has. That's Graziella's radio. She's in the kitchen.'

'Where's your mum gone then?' I said curiously. 'She told mine it was duty calling, or something. Has she got a new part? Is she in a film or anything?'

Tia didn't answer for a moment, and I saw a flash of anger in her blue eyes. Then she said vaguely, 'Oh, you know. Just out,' and she turned her back on me and walked towards her bedroom.

Don't tell me then, I thought. See if I care.

There was no carpet in the gallery, just shiny wooden floorboards, so old and dark they were almost black. I could feel the hard, smooth texture under my feet, and without even thinking, I did a quick routine, just one of our usual practice ones. I didn't have my tap shoes on, of course, only sandals, but they had hard leather soles, and the sound wasn't too bad. It echoed along the gallery and down into the hall below.

Tia stopped dead in her tracks and turned round.

'What's that? What are you doing?'

'Tap. Tap-dancing. I told you before, remember? About my poster? I'm really into it.'

67

I did a bit more, as best I could without my proper shoes on, only a couple of brushes and a roll. Then I spread out my hands and went, 'Da-daa.'

Tia was staring at me, her eyes filled with admiration. I wasn't used to that. People at school are sick of my tap, and I try not to do it there, except with my own little crowd who know me and don't take much notice, but even they tease me sometimes and call me things like 'Happy-tappy' and 'Super-feet'.

'That is just the most brilliant thing,' Tia said, almost reverently. 'It's totally amazing. I couldn't ever do that. Never.'

'Yes, you could.'

I knew she wouldn't be able to, but I couldn't resist proving it to her.

'I'll show you how to do the riff walk,' I said. 'It's dead easy. Watch me. Now, relax your feet and walk naturally. Just ordinarily, in a circle. OK. Squeeze your front knee back. That's the knee trigger. Let the feeling go down into your heel.'

'I don't know what you mean,' Tia said anxiously. 'I can't do it.'

'Yes, you can.' I was sounding like Mrs Litvinov. 'I'll show you again.'

'No, no, I can't!' Tia had stiffened up all over. 'You do it, Carly. Just let me watch. I won't enjoy it if I think I've got to do it too.'

'But a riff walk's not difficult. Look, all you have to—'

'No!' She sounded almost panicky. 'Please! Don't try and teach me. I can never learn anything. Just show me. Do some more and let me watch.'

I shrugged. People don't often ask me to dance for them, and that beautiful gallery with its perfect wooden floor was begging me to have a go. So off I went, into a whole number, slapping my sandals down on the bare boards, hearing the music in my head, showing off to Tia as hard as I possibly could.

When I'd finished she clapped, as if she'd been watching a show.

'Carly, you're incredible! I've never seen anything like it!'

You can't help glowing when someone praises you. I loved it. I grinned at her, wishing I had long hair like hers, to shake out of my eyes in a careless kind of way.

'It's nothing without the proper shoes.' I was trying to sound modest. 'That was only a practice routine anyway. You should see what I'm doing for the display.'

'What display?'

We'd walked on into her bedroom and our feet were now sinking silently into her thick carpet.

'In Torminster. In June. Mrs Litvinov, she's my teacher, she's picked me out to be in the annual show. It's going to be at the town hall.'

'I'll be there,' said Tia. 'Definitely. I've got to see it. You're so good you could dance professionally. On the actual stage.'

I tried to laugh it off.

'Honestly, I'm rubbish really. It's all Mrs Litvinov. She's so brilliant. Mum says she could teach a brick wall to dance.'

We were sitting on her sofa now, curled up at opposite ends, facing each other.

69

'She couldn't teach me,' said Tia. 'I'm absolutely use-less at everything. They've practically given up on me at school. The teachers at school all say I'm lazy, but I'm not. I just freeze up when they try to make me do things. I just know I'll mess everything up and get it wrong.'

She was wearing a blue skirt that day, that looked as if it had stepped right out of a glossy magazine, and over it she had on a skimpy denim jacket, a perfect fit, with little zips and pockets down the front. Her hair was shining like in the TV adverts, and as she spoke she swung it back, so that it brushed against her silk sofa. I felt the snake's tongue of jealousy flicker across my heart.

'So what?' I said, suddenly wanting to be mean. 'You don't need to be good at anything. Everything's been handed to you on a silver plate, thank you very much.'

She shrivelled right up in front of my eyes, and I want-ed to snatch my words back at once.

'I know.' She tried to laugh, pretending she didn't care, though I could see she did. 'I know I've got everything. But the thing is, you see, when it comes to me, myself, I'm nothing. Worthless. Like a useless person or something.'

I sat there feeling terrible. I'd hurt her and I didn't know how to put it right.

'You're not worthless,' I said at last, my voice coming out rougher than I'd intended. 'No one is. Everyone's good at something. Everyone. Mum says that and she ought to know. She's a teacher.'

Tia just shrugged her shoulders.

I felt worse than ever.

'Look,' I said, shifting myself along the sofa, so that I

70

was nearer to her. 'You must be good at something. What's your best subject at school?'

She frowned and rolled her eyes.

'Oh, school,' she said.

'OK. What about – let's see now – things outside school. I know, cooking.'

'I don't know. Graziella never lets me try. She says she's got enough to do without clearing up after me in the kitchen.'

'Sport?'

'I can play tennis a bit, but not really. I just mess about with it. Not nearly good enough for the school tournament anyway.'

I remembered the boots in her cupboard.

'Riding?'

She shuddered.

'I have to when I go to Argentina to stay with Daddy. I've even got my own horse there. I don't dare tell him I hate riding, because he bought Firefly for me specially, and I couldn't bear to hurt his feelings, but I just dread it. Horses simply terrify me. Anyway, I haven't been out to Argentina for years. Firefly's probably got so fat he couldn't even waddle out of the stable.'

I swallowed hard. The jealousy running through me wasn't flickers any more, but real, hot flames. Her own horse! And she didn't even like riding! I pushed the thought away. Tia was a challenge, and I was going to sort her out. One way or another, I had to stop her looking so depressed.

'OK. Look at it another way. Is there anything you really like doing? A hobby or something?'

She looked away from me.

'You'll think I'm silly.'

'Course I won't. Let me guess. You're um – er – you have this weird passion for dangerous reptiles. You keep a cobra in your wardrobe.'

She smiled.

'OK then. You're a trainspotter. You've got a secret store of anoraks.'

'She giggled.

'No? All right. I've got it. You're a closet Elvis impersonator.'

She broke into a shout of laughter. I did too, and we started rolling about on the sofa.

'Elvis!' she gasped. 'White satin and silver glitter!'

'Hair gel and high-heeled boots!'

'Oh my God!'

'We were laughing and hiccuping, our faces bright red and our eyes streaming. We stopped at last. I wasn't going to let her off the hook though.

'What is it then, Tia?' I said. 'What do you like doing?'

'You'll laugh.'

'I won't. I never laugh.'

That set us off again. It was even worse this time. You know how it is when you start laughing and you can't stop, and even though you've forgotten what started it, and it wasn't very funny in the first place, you just go on and on? That's what it was like.

In the end my sides hurt so much I just had to get away. I almost crawled to the bathroom and got myself a drink of water. Then I caught sight of myself in the mirror over the basin, and that sobered me up at once. I looked a total mess. My eyes were streaming, my hair stood on end and my clothes were all ruckled up.

I smoothed myself down and went back to Tia.

She'd stopped laughing too. She was on her knees in front of a big antique-looking chest of drawers, pulling out the bottom one.

She lifted something out and held it up to me.

'I like designing stuff. Clothes. I can't do the real thing, make proper clothes I mean, because Mimi would be bound to find out and tell me I was hopeless, and if I did it at school they'd tease to me to death, so I do it in mini-ature with my old toys. I know it's babyish. I won't mind if you say so. Everyone would think so, if they knew. That's why I keep them hidden in here.'

She was holding her breath as she put a little bear into my hands. I could see that she was terrified that I'd laugh at her.

I took the bear out of her hands. It was just an ordinary teddy, quite sweet, with honey-coloured fur, but it was perfectly dressed in a little suit, with shiny black-satin trousers and a miniature jacket dotted all over with sequins. It was wearing a funny hat, really smart, that perched on top of its head between its ears.

'You didn't make these yourself?' I said. I was dead impressed.

'I did the design and made the patterns and cut them out, and Graziella helped me with the sewing part.' Tia was watching me anxiously. 'She's brilliant at it. She trained as a dressmaker actually. I used to just watch her, but I'm learning how to do it myself now. She doesn't say

73

anything to Mimi because she really enjoys doing it too. Anyway, she says it keeps me quiet and out of her way. Look, here's another.'

She took a fluffy dog out of the drawer. It was a weird green colour, and you'd never have looked twice at it except for its clothes. Tia had made a sort of evening dress out of a piece of crimson silk. It had straps, a little padded bust and tiny rosebuds sewn round the neck. It was strange, but clever and sweet too.

'They're silly aren't they?' she said. 'I knew you'd think so. I only do it for fun. I know I'm useless at it.'

I was still turning the dog over in my hands.

'You mean you designed these clothes, and made patterns, and cut out the material and everything? Tia, I'm so impressed. They're so cool. I could never do anything like this. They're just – they're perfect.'

She looked pleased and unbelieving and embarrassed. Then she turned back to the drawer.

'This is my best one,' she said.

She put into my hands the most beautiful doll I'd ever seen. It wasn't a baby, like most dolls are, more a miniature woman. I don't suppose it was ever meant to be actually played with. Her face was delicately tinted, and her long dark hair was pinned up in neat waves under a little round hat. She was wearing a black dress, satin, with lace on it, like something out of the 1920s. Exactly my kind of thing.

Tia felt about in the drawer and pulled out more little clothes, some sheets of paper, snippets of cloth and a couple of notebooks. I picked up one of these and leafed through the pages. They were covered with drawings of clothes, evening dresses, historical costumes, coats, skirts, hats.

'You did all these?' I said, waving them at her. 'Out of your head?'

'Yes.'

She was so pleased at the admiration in my voice that her cheeks started going pink.

'Move over Versace. Your time is past and gone,' I said, and I meant it too. 'I don't get it, Tia. How can you sit there, saying you're useless, when you can design amazing stuff like this?'

She sat back on her heels and looked at me shyly.

'It's just dolls,' she said. 'Silly bits of nothing. Like me, really.'

I was suddenly furiously irritated. I wanted to shout at her, Listen to yourself! Stop grovelling! You sound totally pathetic! But then I saw the look on her face.

You mean it, I thought. You really do feel like that. Like nothing, and a shiver ran through me. I looked down at the doll's painted face and its wide blue eyes stared blindly up into mine. I didn't want to hold it any more. I put it down on the sofa. It looked like an abandoned dancer in its little black 1920s' dress, with the long rope of miniature pearls round its neck.

At that very moment a brilliant idea, the best I'd ever had in the whole of my life, was opening like a flower inside my head.

'I want you to do something for me, Tia,' I said, and my voice sounded squeaky with excitement. 'I want you to design my costume for the display. Say you will. You've got to. I really, really mean it.'

75

8

There's one thing about me that you should know. When I make up my mind about doing something, and go all out for it, I usually manage to get it done. Mum says I'd have a great career as a head teacher. Dad says I'll make some bloke's life a roller-coaster mixture of heaven and hell. No comment on what Sam and Lauren say.

I had to work through Tia's absolute refusal, then her panic attack, then about a million feeble excuses. At last she said, 'Suppose I do. Suppose I say yes. It'll be a total failure and everyone will laugh at you.'

I said, 'They won't. It'll be a smash hit, you'll see.'

After ages and ages, she took a deep breath as if she was trying to find some courage in the bottom of her lungs.

'All right,' she said, 'I'll try.'

Then she looked almost giddy with fright.

'Yes!' I shouted, punching the air. 'Next thing is you'll have to come home with me, and talk it over with Mum.'

Then I realized what I'd done. I'd invited Tia, the princess of Paradise End, to witness for herself the horrors of McQuarrie family life. There was no going back though. Her eyes had lit up with excitement. It was as if I'd offered her a trip to the moon. A horrible feeling was settling in my stomach.

'Tia,' I said, 'you don't have to do this. You don't know what you're letting yourself in for. Once you've seen our house you'll never speak to me again. Trust me. I'm telling you the truth.'

She jumped up.

'Let's go and tell Graziella. We could go round now.'

She was still holding her beautiful doll. I had the weirdest feeling that its round china face had become a miniature version of mine. I could just see myself in the lovely clothes she was wearing. I could almost feel the long rope of pearls dangling from my own neck and hear the faint swishing noise of the material touching my legs. I was longing so much to look like her that I was even prepared to go through with the awfulness of taking Tia home.

'I'll have to ask Mum,' I said. 'I don't know whether she'll have enough tea for us.'

Tia pushed her slim little mobile into my hands.

'Call her then.' She sounded almost bossy for once.

Mum picked up the phone on its third ring. I could tell she was in the kitchen, doing the ironing. I could practically see the mounds of clothes all round her, and the mess of drying up on the draining board.

'It's me,' I said.

'Carly? Are you OK?'

'Of course I'm OK.' I knew I was being snappy, but I was too nervous to care. I cleared my throat. 'Mum, Tia wants to come round. Is there enough for us both for tea? She's going to – I mean, I've asked her to help with my costume for the display.'

'Oh.' I could imagine Mum's eyebrows rising right up into her hairline. 'Yes, love. Of course you can bring her. I'll get another pizza out of the freezer.'

She sounded really pleased. She's always like that about my friends. She gets nosy and wants to meet them. The warning bells that I'd been trying to ignore started jangling away in my head again. I know my family. When they get fascinated by something they're on to it like dogs on a bone. They'd be all over Tia, pumping her for stuff about Paradise End, and the swimming pool and the tennis court, and all the things I'd bragged about, and when they did I'd die of embarrassment.

I switched off the phone. Tia was already off the sofa and halfway to the door.

'Come on,' she said to me over her shoulder. 'We'll go and tell Graziella. She's in the kitchen.'

I followed her into the gallery. I couldn't imagine how I'd practically danced my socks off there, just a little while ago. My feet felt like lead.

What was it about Paradise End? Why did it always reflect my mood? A little while ago I'd felt its beauty hold on to me like a spell. Now the house seemed to harden itself against me. The portraits on the walls looked down jeeringly. The doors round the hall, all closed now, seemed to be deliberately shutting me out.

Tia raced down the stairs and darted under the gallery at the back of the hall. I followed her slowly. We were in a long corridor now. She ran along it. At the far end was a door covered with green cloth. She pushed it open and jumped down the two steps behind it.

We were in a vast kitchen, the biggest outside school

I'd ever seen. It was all shiny metal and white cupboard doors, hard surfaces, gleaming steel and polished wood. As clean as a hospital, almost.

No one was there.

Tia called out, 'Graziella?' and a door at the far end opened.

I supposed I'd expected Graziella to be short and round, with a mob cap on her head, a long dress, a big white apron going all the way down to her feet, and a wooden spoon in her hand, like a cook in a fairy story. She wasn't like that at all. She was quite young for a start – well, much younger looking than Mum anyway – and really pretty, with curly dark hair and a great figure. She was wearing jeans and a yellow T-shirt, and she was carrying a bulging plastic carrier bag.

'Hello,' she said. 'You are Carly, no?'

She had a thick Italian accent and quite a deep voice.

'Listen, Grazi,' Tia said breathlessly. 'Carly and I are going to her house for supper. Do you mind? We won't need to eat anything here.'

Graziella frowned and said something in Italian. Tia broke into a stream of Italian too. I couldn't believe my ears. None of us at school can say more than three words even in French and we've been learning it for ages. I was so impressed I stood and listened with my mouth hanging open.

At last Graziella shrugged and said, 'Is far, your house, Carly?'

'Just down the road.' My voice sounded hollow.

'I come with you, to see,' Graziella said. 'Mrs Dixie, she no like Tia going out somewhere she no sure about.'

That made me frown. My family might be dead embarrassing, but there was no reason for anyone to be suspicious of us. We might be untidy, but we're quite clean actually. You wouldn't catch diseases at our house. But before I could make a comeback, Tia said, 'Be with you in half a tick, Carly. I promised Graziella I'd take my mobile so I can call her to fetch me when I want to come home.'

'It's OK,' I began feebly. 'You can use the phone at . . .' But Tia had already run out of the kitchen.

I looked round to see that Graziella was studying me, with her head on one side.

'So, Carly,' she said. 'You live close to here, isn't it?'

'Yeah,' I said. 'Just down the road.'

'Tia, she need a very nice friend.' Graziella was looking at me as if I was a signboard she was trying to read. 'If you come sometimes, she will be very happy.'

I felt I was being checked out, and I didn't like it much.

'Anyone can see she's lonely,' I said. 'So why doesn't she invite any friends from her school?'

A peculiar look crossed Graziella's face.

'Mrs Dixie, she is . . .' she began.

I could hear Tia already, running back towards the green-cloth door.

'It's OK, Graziella,' I said quickly. 'I won't get her into trouble or anything. She'll be OK with me.'

I don't know what made me say that. My words seemed to echo around that huge kitchen like a solemn promise.

Graziella smiled.

At least she seems to be on Tia's side, I thought, more than her mother is anyway.

*

It was odd, walking down our street with Tia and Graziella, a strange mixing of two worlds. To my surprise, when we stopped outside number thirty-four, our house, Graziella looked up at it as if she really approved of it. I could see her taking in Sam's old bike by the front door, and Lauren's toys propped up on the window sill in our bedroom.

'You got brothers and sisters?' she said, looking pleased.

'Yes,' I said gloomily, fishing in my pocket for my door-key.

'OK.' Graziella turned away. 'You call me, Tia, when you ready to come home. Have a nice time.'

She walked off, back towards Paradise End, her high-heeled mules clicking on the pavement as she went.

'Right,' I said to Tia. 'This is it. You're going to regret it, honestly. Madhouse city. Dumpsville. It's more civilized at the zoo.'

I wished I hadn't said that then, because Tia started looking terrified. Funnily enough, the sudden paleness of her face made me feel a bit better.

'No, really,' I said. 'It's not that bad. They're all going to love you. Too much. That's what I'm afraid of,' and I took a deep breath, shoved the key into the lock and pushed open the door.

'Welcome,' I said, 'to chaos.'

9

Isn't it just my luck that everyone's around this evening? And isn't it even worse that Dad's taken it into his head to mend the castor on the sofa in the sitting room (the only room that ever looks halfway nice) and has turned the whole place upside down? And would you believe that Sam has been out mud-wrestling (he calls it playing rugby) and his filthy clothes are scattered over the hall floor?

I look into the sitting room and see Dad's backside as he's leaning right over the sofa, so I quickly shut it again. Then we pick our way over Sam's clothes towards the kitchen.

Mum's standing at the table, folding up my tatty old pyjamas. I've never noticed before how small our kitchen is, and how amazingly messy. I mean, every work surface is cluttered up with jam-jars and rolls of kitchen paper and broken gadgets and school notes.

'Hi, Tia,' says Mum, pushing a strand of limp permed hair off her shiny forehead. 'Pleased to meet you.'

'Hello, Mrs McQuarrie,' Tia answers faintly. 'It's awfully – awfully nice of you to . . .'

Her voice fades away.

The door crashes open and Sam bursts in.

'When's tea, Mum? I'm starving.' He sees me. 'Wotcha, Spiky-top. Thought you'd gone off to eat caviar with your posh friend.' I shut my eyes and want to curl up into a very, very little ball.

Sam sees Tia. He wiggles his hips and grins at her.

'Wa-hey! Look who's here! It's little Miss Muffet. Got bad news for you, Miss M. I'm the spider.'

He makes his eyes go googly, holds his hand up palm side down and wiggles his fingers. I haven't dared look at Tia since she came into the house, but I glance sideways at her now. She's pressed her back against the fridge, and she's looking at him, fascinated, as if his hand really had turned into a tarantula. I notice all over again how perfect and expensive her clothes are, and I quickly look away.

Mum puts a pile of clean ironed clothes into Sam's hands.

'Take these upstairs,' she says, 'and put them *away*. In *drawers*. Do not leave them on the floor. Do not dump them on your bed. Now girls, give us a hand. Tia, there's a cloth in the sink. Wipe the table down, will you? Carly, get out the cutlery and plates. The pizzas must be done by now.'

Tia darts forward, really keen to be useful, but awkward too, as if she doesn't know quite what to do. I wait for her to finish with the table before I set it. I can see she's not used to cleaning things. She dabs at the surface and misses lots of smeary bits.

Mum goes to the door and yells, 'Tea's ready!' There's a sound like charging rhinos, and the kitchen's a confused mass of people and chairs and then we're all sitting round the table.

Lauren, the little creep, has snatched the chair next to Tia's. She hasn't taken her eyes off her since she came into the room. She's trying to look cute, and almost succeeding. I scowl as I see Tia look down and smile at her.

Dad washes his hands at the sink, turns round and says, 'Hello, young lady. You must be Carly's new friend.'

'Yes,' Tia says shyly. 'How do you do, Mr McQuarrie?'

Her voice is so posh I hold my breath, waiting for Sam to burst out laughing. He nearly does, but catches Mum's eye. She frowns him down.

'Ham and pineapple, or – what's this? Cheese and mushroom,' says Dad, his knife poised above the pizzas. No one says anything. They're all too busy staring at Tia.

'Ham and pineapple,' I say loudly. 'Please.' And I pass my plate.

'Any pee in that pot?' Sam says, passing his mug to Mum.

I've taken my first mouthful of pizza, and I choke on it.

'Sam!' I hiss at him.

Mum casts up her eyes.

'Don't take any notice of him, Tia,' she says, pouring out the tea. 'He's just a revolting adolescent.'

Tia's cheeks have gone scarlet. She doesn't know where to look.

'I'm not the only adolescent around here,' Sam says. 'Have you started shaving under your arms yet, Carly? Because if you have, I'm warning you, one touch of my razor and you're dead meat.'

I'm the one who's scarlet now. I want to explode, burst into tears, sink through floor, kill Sam and die. Normally I'd go for him, big time, but I can't bear to show myself up in front of Tia. I can only sit there and suffer. Dad chips in.

'That's *enough*,' he says sharply, pointing his knife at Sam.

Everyone's eating. I've never noticed before how crude my family is, how they grab at things and spill things, and make slurpy noises, and drop things on the floor.

Thank God, Lauren's silent for once. She seems to be totally smitten by Tia. She takes a couple of bites of pizza and loses interest in it. The two middle fingers of her left hand creep into her mouth (Mum keeps claiming she's eight years old, but how many kids of her age still do that, if you please?) and with her right hand she starts stroking and stroking the silky material of Tia's sleeve.

'Stop that, Lauren!' I snap. 'Leave Tia alone.'

Tia has been eating tiny bits of pizza really neatly. She shakes her hair back and gives a little laugh.

'I don't mind,' she says. 'I like it. Really. Lauren's so sweet.'

Sam belches loudly.

'Sweet? Lauren?' He rolls his eyes. 'Oh man. Sweet like nitric acid.'

Lauren's wearing her hard-soled shoes. She kicks Sam expertly on the shin. He leans under the table, grabs her legs and pulls. She screams and starts to disappear, snatching at the edge of the table as she goes under. It begins to tip. Plates and glasses are sliding about. World War Three's about to break out. The kitchen's going to be nuked and there's absolutely nothing I can do about it. I put my head in my hands. I've never been so humiliated in my entire life. I hate Sam and Lauren with a deep and total and everlasting passion. I'm going to run away as soon as I possibly can and start a new life in Australia. I'll never be able to look Tia in the face again.

'Sam!' roars Dad. 'Stop that at once!'

The table rights itself. Lauren slides back up on to her chair. Sam grins.

'Sorry, Dad.'

'What is the matter with you today?' Mum says crossly. She smiles apologetically at Tia. 'He's not usually this bad. Not quite anyway.'

'Sorry,' Sam says again. 'I'm really, really happy, that's all. I've had some great news.'

'Oh?' says Dad. 'Let me guess. You've made the first fifteen at last.'

'You passed your maths exam,' says Mum.

'You got Ellie Smithers to kiss you back,' says Lauren.

It's Sam's turn to go scarlet. Lauren is triumphant.

'Ellie Smithers! Ellie Smithers!' she chants.

Sam tries to ignore her.

'I've got myself a job,' he says. 'It's really good. Weekends and evenings, and only now and then. It's with Jepson's.'

'What's Jepson's?' says Lauren, her eyes all sharp and nosy.

Sam ignores her. He's looking at Mum, who's frowning.

'They do catering, don't they? For parties?' she says. 'What sort of a job are they offering you?'

'I'm going to be a waiter,' says Sam triumphantly. 'I'm going to walk around in a little white jacket and black bow tie like in the films and wow all the girls. It's dead easy. All I've got to do is pass drinks and stuff round on trays.'

Mum's looking doubtful.

'What about the late nights? Your school-work?'

'Lighten up, Mum.' Sam's beginning to look annoyed. 'All my mates have got jobs. It won't even be every weekend, and I can always say I can't do it.'

Dad chips in.

'Good for you, Sam.' He looks over at Mum. He doesn't like disagreeing with her in front of us, but I can see the fact that he approves is bringing her round to it. 'Sounds like a great idea to me. We'll be able to charge you rent at last.'

He grins to show he doesn't mean it.

Sam's stuffing a massive piece of pizza into his mouth, but he still goes on speaking through it.

'Thought I'd spend it on driving lessons.'

That wipes the smile off Dad's face. Mum can see an argument's going to break out.

'Guess what's for dessert?' she says.

We don't usually have a dessert, but today Mum's got our favourite chocolate ice-cream roll out of the freezer for a special treat. While I clear the pizza plates away, she dollops it into our bowls. Lauren watches, her eyes like slits, in case anyone gets more that anyone else.

No one talks much while they get stuck into their ice cream. I'm doing what I usually do, working round the edge of the lump with my spoon, then licking it off slowly, letting the cold, creamy sweetness slither down my throat.

Then I catch sight of Tia. She's taken a couple of delicate little mouthfuls and stopped. She's pushed her bowl to one side with a sort of grand unconcern. She doesn't seem to realize how special this is, and how everyone's dying for more.

I feel like a total yob, like a caveman or a barbarian or something. I slow down and try to take smaller mouthfuls of ice cream too, and I have to look away from Dad, who suddenly looks like a greedy bear, and from Mum, who looks dumpy and like a kind of sweet-o-holic.

Thank God, the meal's over at last. Sam jumps up.

'Got something for you, Spiky-head,' he says to me, barging out of the room.

I sit and wait, numb with horror. This has been the most awful meal of my entire life. It can't possibly get any worse. Sam can't do anything more to me now. He's totally destroyed me already.

He's back a minute later, and he plonks my old Walkman and a stack of tapes down beside me.

'I've mended this thing for you,' he says. 'Took hours. Goes like a dream now though. And I taped all those tracks you wanted. Got some more for you too.'

He starts singing, in an awful tuneless voice, '*Cry me a river . . .*'

Suddenly he looks funny, and quite handsome, and sort of cool. For a moment, I almost forget the last ghastly half-hour.

'Wow, Sam,' I say, 'you're a dude.'

'Right,' says Mum, heaving herself to her feet. 'Washing up.'

'It's Carly's turn,' Lauren says. 'I'll take Tia upstairs.'

'Carly's excused today,' Mum says. 'It's you and Sam, Lauren.'

Lauren's face sets itself and I know we're in for a whining session. I grab Tia's hand, get her out of the kitchen and slam the door behind us. I lean against the door of the cupboard under the stairs and feel myself trembling all over.

'Look,' I say, 'I'm really, really sorry. I did warn you. I know you'll want to go home now, and never see me again, but . . .'

Tia's staring at me, her eyes wide open.

'What on earth are you talking about, Carly? I think your family's great. They're lovely.' A slight blush is spreading up her cheeks. 'What's Sam – I mean, is he still at school? Where does he go?'

I'm not thick. I'm quite sharp actually, when it comes to these things, and I can tell that the weirdest, whackiest thing has happened, something I'd never have believed in a million years. Anastasia Lucille Braithwaite Krukovsky actually fancies my revolting brother Samuel John McQuarrie.

If Tia had been anyone else, like one of my friends at school, or Lizzie or Simone at tap, I'd have had a go at her about Sam, but I knew better than to try it out on Tia. Here, in our noisy, quarrelling house, she seemed almost fragile, like her own porcelain doll.

I couldn't remember, as I opened my bedroom door, whether I'd left it looking like a tip or not. Luckily, I hadn't, for once. My side was OK. Lauren's was as messy as usual, though, with her Barbie stuff scattered all over the place.

'Oh! It's Barbie!' Tia said, picking up the revolting thing and stroking its golden hair. 'One of my nannies gave me one when I was little. I adored it. Mimi hated it and made me throw it away. She said it was . . .' She stopped and bit her lip, embarrassed.

'Naff,' I said, nodding. 'She was dead right.'

Tia put the doll back on Lauren's bed and turned to look at my Ginger-and-Fred poster.

'It's beautiful.' She looked almost reverent. 'But I don't think I could . . .'

I read her mind.

'No, that's not how I want my costume to look. Ginger's dress is too grand and fussy. I want mine to be like your doll. Clean lines. Simple. Honestly, Tia, it's so lovely, so elegant and sort of classy.'

A door slammed downstairs and a shout of laughter from Sam wafted up from below. Tia looked towards the door. Banging noises came from the sitting room, right underneath our bedroom, where Dad must have been turning the sofa back upright again. Mum's voice was booming out over the others as she tried to make herself heard on the phone.

I began to feel embarrassed again.

'Dad keeps saying we ought to move to a bigger house. You can hardly turn round in this one. I never get any space to be on my own.'

She looked round at me, her thin, flying eyebrows lifted in surprise.

'You're so lucky,' she said.

'You're having me on,' I said, annoyed. I couldn't believe she was sincere. 'What did you say that for?'

She could see she'd irritated me. I was beginning to understand how sensitive she was to all my moods.

'If I lived in this house, I wouldn't get scared at night,' she said at last.

I thought of her huge bedroom. It had been fine in the daytime, but I suddenly realized that to be there in the dark, on your own, to hear the wind rattling the windows, the floorboards creaking outside in the long gallery, and the tick of the old clock echoing round the high-roofed hall below would be horribly scary. I knew, though, that wasn't the only thing she'd meant. I wanted to get her to tell me more, but I stopped myself.

People aren't tin cans, Mum says sometimes. *You can't prise them open with a tin opener. You remember that, Carly, before you go barging in and trampling all over people's finer feelings.*

You've probably guessed by now that 'tactful' isn't exactly my middle name. I was beginning to realize, though, that I'd have to learn some tact if I was going to get on with Tia. She was like a wild animal. She'd shy away from me if I came in too close. I was starting to see that I'd have to be patient for once, and let her tell me stuff when she wanted to, without me forcing it out of her. It was a new experience for me.

'Your mother looks really kind,' she burst out suddenly.

'Kind?' I thought about it. 'She gets furious sometimes. And she's usually on Lauren's side. It makes me mad, I can tell you.'

'Your father's nice too.'

'He calls me Twinkle-toes. I hate it.'

She shook her head.

'You've just got no idea how lucky you are,' she said.

'What's your dad like then?' I said, letting my curiosity have its way.

91

She looked out of the window, and I felt her pull back from me again.

'I'm supposed to see him once a year, in the summer, but something usually turns up to stop me going. Mimi messes up the plans, or says I'm ill or something, and won't let me go.'

'I don't get it. Why does he let her? He's your dad, isn't he?'

She stared at me.

'You don't know Mimi. Anyway . . .'

'Anyway what?'

'He's married again. How do I know he really wants to see me? And Lucia, that's his new wife, I've never met her, but she'll probably hate me. You know what stepmothers are supposed to be like. She'll be obsessed with the baby anyway.'

'What baby? You mean your brother?'

'My – brother. Yes.'

I nearly said, *You know what, Tia? You've got to toughen yourself up. Be a bit braver. Get a bit more confidence in yourself,* but I didn't. All I said was, 'She'll like you if you play with the baby and keep him out of her hair. Mums always do. What's his name anyway?'

'Jojo. But it's really Joachim.

I had a whole heap more questions I was dying to ask, but then the door opened and Lauren crashed in. Trust Lauren. I mean, that is *so* typical. You're having a really intimate conversation with your own exclusive friend when little Miss Sneaky-ears Hide-as-thick-as-a-warthog comes barging in, nose quivering, trying to sniff out everyone else's business.

'Mum says you're planning Carly's costume for the display. Say I can help. Please, Tia!'

'Look.' I turn on her savagely. 'We've got an agreement here, remember? Whoever's got a friend round gets to have some space. The other one goes away, or at least shuts up and doesn't interfere and lets them get on with it. OK? *OK?* Or has your pigeon-sized brain shredded that particular bit of information?'

'It's all right, Carly.' Tia's voice breaks in. 'Let her stay. You'll be really quiet and let us get on with it, won't you, Lauren? If you do, I'll make an evening dress for your Barbie. Midnight-blue velvet with a sequinned jacket. Would you like that?'

Lauren's speechless. All she can do is nod. She tiptoes to her bed and sits on it, absolutely still, sucks her cheeks right in and watches us, wide-eyed and silent.

'Tia,' I say, slightly put out, 'you don't have to waste your time on crappy Barbie dolls.'

I stop. I've suddenly remembered the one her mother made her throw away.

'I'd love to, honestly.' I can see she means it. 'Perhaps we'd better start. Have you got any paper, Carly? And a pencil?'

I couldn't believe how brilliant Tia was. She sat back on her heels and thought for a bit, then she leaned over the paper and started to draw. She rubbed it all out lots of times and started again, but at last there it was – the dress I wanted, not exactly like the one her doll was wearing, but even better. Right for a girl. Right for me.

I held my breath while she worked on it, watching it take shape on the paper.

It would fall, I could see, in a straight, clean line of black silk from shoulder to knee, fitting, but not hugging too closely. She seemed to know without me saying that I wouldn't want the whole world to see how flat my chest was. She'd drawn in a big white flower just under one shoulder, a real touch of glamour, and a long string of beads to give a hint of the 1920s. I'd look amazing in it, I knew I would.

I looked up once and caught Lauren's eye. She was sitting unnaturally still, holding her Barbie close to her chest. She looked so funny, not daring to move an inch, as if she was frozen stiff, that I nearly let out a laugh.

Then Mum put her head round the door.

'How are you girls getting on? It's so quiet up here I thought you must have passed out or something.'

'Look, Mum.'

I held out Tia's sketch. Mum took the paper and studied it. I could see respect in her eyes.

'This is lovely, Tia,' she said, in the kind of voice she uses at school when one of her dim kids has surprised her. 'You've got a talent for design, I can see.'

'Can you do it, Mum?' I was desperate to know. 'Can you make it?'

Mum's mouth twisted to one side.

'I'm not sure, quite frankly. It's the sort of really simple thing that's not easy to get right. It's all in the cut, and without a pattern . . .'

'I'll ask Graziella to help me,' said Tia. 'She won't mind doing it, I know she won't.'

'Graziella's Tia's housekeeper,' I said, enjoying the grand sound of the words.

Mum's eyebrows snapped together, and I could see the words 'getting above yourself' zipping through her mind.

'It needs to be cut on the cross, that's what's tricky,' Tia said, sounding brilliantly professional, though I had no idea what she meant. 'Graziella's awfully good at sewing. She could make the pattern easily, and do the cutting. She was a dressmaker once. She—'

'Tia.' Mum cut right across her. She was frowning with disapproval. 'We can't possibly ask your mother's housekeeper to put in all the work that's needed for this. She's got her own work to do.'

'It's OK, Mrs McQuarrie,' Tia said nervously, as if Mum was a cross teacher at school or something. 'Graziella and I often make things together. She really likes doing it. And my mother won't even know. She's never there. She wouldn't care at all.'

The obstinate look that I knew only too well was creeping over Mum's face. When she thinks something's wrong, you can't budge her, whatever you say. It's so irritating it always makes me want to go right out and do the other thing.

'I'm sorry, but it's not right to deceive your mother and exploit her employee,' she said firmly. 'I'll have to—'

Downstairs, the front doorbell rang.

'I'll get it!' shouted Sam.

We all stopped to listen. A woman's murmured voice floated up to us.

'There's Graziella now,' said Tia, looking disappointed.

95

'I didn't think she'd be coming so soon. I suppose I'll have to go.'

Mum went out of the room and we followed her down the stairs. Sam stepped back from the front door. Graziella, looking worried, stood on the step, and behind her, by the front gate, I saw a heavily built man in a black suit. He looked like a bouncer.

'Tia, you must come home with me now,' Graziella said urgently. 'Mr Braithwaite has come. He is angry because you are not at home. He says I have to take you back at once.'

A look of alarm swept across Tia's face.

'What's Hollins doing here?' she said, looking at the man outside.

'Nothing. Not to worry, Tia. Mr Braithwaite sent him with the car to fetch you. Come, you must hurry.'

Tia was halfway out of the door already.

'I'm frightfully sorry, Mrs McQuarrie,' she said, looking over my head at Mum. 'My uncle gets into a terrible panic sometimes. Thank you so much for having me. It was awfully good of you. I've had a lovely time.'

She sounded like a little girl at a birthday party, repeating lines she'd learned off by heart.

'But you can't just go, Tia!' I said. 'What are we going to do? About the dress?'

'Graziella and I will work on it,' said Tia. She smiled coaxingly at Graziella. 'I just know you're going to love this, Grazi. I'll tell you all about it. Carly, can you – I mean could you possibly come over tomorrow, so we can take your measurements?'

'Tia! *Come!*' Graziella said even more urgently.

'I'll call you,' Tia said over her shoulder, as she stepped into the back of the huge black car that was waiting at the kerb ouside our house. Mr Hollins, who had been holding the door open for her, looked up and down the street as he slammed it shut, and got into the driving seat, with Graziella in the front beside him. Then he drove off quickly up the road.

10

'*Well*,' said Mum as she closed the front door. 'Very cool, I must say.'

'Who's cool? What do you mean?' I said sharply.

Mum looked at me, and I could see she was about to start. Normally, I punch out first before she gets going, but I wasn't in the mood for a row.

'Mr Braithwaite must be her uncle,' I said, to sidetrack her. 'You wouldn't believe what his nickname is.'

'Something weird, I know,' Mum said thoughtfully. 'Ice or Snow or something.'

I could hear Sam snort behind me and Dad, who had come to the sitting room door, laughed.

'It's Frost, actually,' I said, feeling quite defensive.

'Frost! You have to be kidding!' said Sam, but not very loudly. I could tell, actually, that he'd been dead impressed by Mr Hollins, and especially by the big car.

'Frost! That's it!' Mum's face cleared. 'I knew I'd seen it somewhere. There's a piece about them all – it even mentions Tia, I think – in the magazine I picked up in the staffroom last week. I didn't connect her with it at the time. Now what did I do with it? I tried to find it yesterday.'

Dad went into the sitting room and came back with a magazine in his hands.

'This it? I found it under the sofa.'

She snatched it from him.

'Oh, thank goodness. Carole wants it back. Now where was that piece? Yes, here we are. Page twenty-four.'

We all looked over her shoulder. There was a grainy photograph of a girl with long blonde hair in a bikini that could have been Tia. It was hard to tell. It must have been taken from miles away with one of those really powerful telephoto lenses. The girl was sitting on the edge of a swimming pool in what looked like a tropical place, with palm trees in the background. She was dangling her legs in the water. Under the headline, *BRIDES OF THE FUTURE: the world's most eligible girls*, it said:

Still a little young for wedding bells, but here's one we'll all be hearing about soon. Anastasia Krukovsky, the sole heiress to one of the world's greatest private fortunes, was born with the biggest jewel-encrusted spoon in her mouth that any lucky little girl could wish for. Her mother, 'Dixie' Braithwaite, had a short-lived film career, which fizzled out almost as soon as it had begun. The wild parties she gave filled the gossip columns a decade or more ago. Not that Dixie (forty-five) needs the support of a career. She is twin sister to the banker 'Frost' Braithwaite, and co-heiress of the fabulous Braithwaite fortune.

Joshua Braithwaite, the twins' great-grandfather, started life as a penniless labourer. He rose from rags to riches a century and a half ago, founding a coal-and-steel empire that buried acres of the Midlands under bricks and mortar. Unless

Anastasia's Uncle Frost decides to marry at last and produce an heir, the little blonde beauty with the big blue eyes will scoop the lot.

Dixie's family made their pile out of muck and sweat, but Anastasia's dad (now divorced from Dixie) has a touch of class. Count Rudolf ('Rudi') Krukovsky, ex-playboy Argentinian racing-stud owner, is a descendant of a bona-fide aristocratic Russian family. And, as the photograph shows, young Anastasia looks every inch a countess. So polish up your manners, boys, and dust down your best clothes. This little sleeping beauty will soon be looking for her handsome prince!

It felt really peculiar, reading all that stuff in a magazine about someone I actually knew, with a photo and everything. It made Tia seem a long way away.

'She's like a film star herself, or royalty or something,' I said. The girl in the picture seemed unreal to me, as if the magazine had made her up.

'Poor little thing,' said Mum. 'I wouldn't wish the paparazzi on my worst enemy.'

Lauren seemed to have come out of her trance. She'd trailed down the stairs and was sitting on the bottom step, holding her doll.

'Tia's not a poor thing. She's a princess and she's going to make my Barbie an evening dress,' she said. 'Midnight-blue velvet with a sequinned jacket.'

Mum looked sceptical and shook her head. I knew the look on her face.

'She *is*,' insisted Lauren. 'She *promised*.'

'You don't like her, Mum, do you? What's the matter with her? Tia's a really nice person. She knows she's not a brainbox. She's really modest. Not stuck up at all. She was lovely about how awful it was at teatime.'

'Oh?' There were bright-red spots in Mum's cheeks. 'And what was so awful about teatime?'

'Mum! Sam was *horrible*! You know he was. I was so embarrassed I wanted to lie down and die.'

'If you're invited to other people's houses,' Mum said, 'you have to take them as you find them. I noticed that the food wasn't up to Miss Tia's standards. She left most of her pizza and hardly tasted her chocolate roll. Two mouthfuls, then she pushed it away as if it was muck. That's what I call rude.'

'She didn't mean to be rude!' My face was red now. 'She's not used to families like ours. Her mother doesn't have to cook and do the ironing and housework and everything, and go out to work like you do. She doesn't understand.'

Mum's eyebrows snapped together, and I was bracing myself for a real row, but then I saw that she was forcing herself to calm down.

'Look, love,' she said, 'I've got nothing against Tia. She seems like a nice kid. Not overly blessed in the brains department, perhaps, but . . .'

'She speaks Italian,' I muttered, not wanting to spark her off again. 'Perfectly.'

'I dare say.' Mum didn't seem impressed.

Dad had been half listening while he cleared up his tools from the sitting-room floor. Now he came out into the hall.

'I was glad to see they'd got a proper security man on the job,' he said. 'If there's that kind of money involved, the kid's a sitting duck for kidnappers. I hope they've taken proper precautions on alarms and security systems up at Paradise End. I don't like the idea of you getting mixed up in all of that, Carly.'

I was hopping up and down by now.

'What are you talking about? Tia's my *friend*! I'm not going to get mixed up in anything! Why don't you be honest for once and say what you really think? You're jealous, that's all it is. You know we live in a crappy house at the crappy end of a crappy village, and we can never afford to buy nice clothes or have a decent car, and you're ashamed of it, just like I am.'

There was an awful silence. Dad looked at Mum. He looked a bit sad. She just looked tired. I felt really, really bad.

'Carly, that's not very nice and it's also very silly,' Mum said in a hurt voice. 'I don't dislike Tia at all. I just can't quite work out what's going on inside that cool little head of hers. I grant you, her manners are perfect – except when it comes to finishing off what's on her plate – which is only what you'd expect, with all the money that's no doubt been spent on her education, and she seems perfectly sweet and good-natured. A little too sweet, perhaps. I can't quite make up my mind about her. I've known girls like Tia who can be quite sly and manipulative. On the other hand, she might be so keen to please because she's desperate for affection. I just think you should be careful, that's all. I don't want you to fling yourself into a situation with these people, and then be rejected when they decide they've had enough.'

She was making me see red again.

'You don't know what you're talking about!' I shouted at her. 'You just don't understand!'

I couldn't take any more of it. I raced upstairs to our bedroom, slammed the door and pulled the chest of drawers across it, so that Lauren couldn't come in and see me cry.

11

It took me the rest of the evening to calm down, and the next morning, which was Sunday, I was still seething. It was worse because I was feeling guilty too. I couldn't believe I'd said such cruel, awful things to Mum and Dad. I hated myself for that.

Everyone does their own thing in our house on Sunday morning. Mum sleeps in. Dad does too, when he's not on duty. Sam never gets up till gone one o'clock. Lauren watches TV. I do what I like.

I woke with a start, quite early for me, at ten o'clock, and lay in bed waiting for the phone to ring. When it did, I shot downstairs as if an axe-murderer was after me and snatched the receiver off the hook.

I knew it would be Tia, and it was.

'Can you come over, Carly?' she said. 'This morning? How soon?'

'Now. I've just got to get dressed.'

I ran back upstairs and put on my nicest casual clothes. There wasn't a lot of choice, but I did my best. It was hot that day, so I didn't need a sweater or anything, just my favourite denim trousers and my little cut-off white top. My hair was the problem as usual, sticking up all over my head like a black bottlebrush.

By the time I was ready, Mum was up. Her bedroom door was open and I could hear her moving around. I went downstairs and opened the sitting-room door.

'Tell Mum,' I said loudly to Lauren, who was sitting on the floor sucking her fingers like a toddler and gawping at the TV, 'that Tia's called, and I've gone up to Paradise End. I don't know when I'll be back.'

Lauren didn't budge. Mum had come out on to the landing above, and I knew she'd heard me.

'Did you get that, Lauren?' I said very clearly. 'Tell Mum. I'm going to Paradise End. I'll probably be there all day.'

Lauren only grunted. She hadn't taken in a single word. But Mum had. I heard her slippered feet move towards the top of the stairs.

'Goodbye!' I called and went out of the front door.

I waited outside for a moment, in case she came after me, but she didn't, so I ran off up the road.

For the first time, there was no Tia to let me in between the big steely gates. I stood uncertainly, looking through the bars, not knowing what to do. Then, from out of one of the garages on the left of the wide gravel drive, came the bouncer-looking man, Mr Hollins.

He saw me standing there and walked up towards me, his bulging arms swinging, the thick crêpe soles of his heavy black boots crunching on the gravel.

'What do you want?'

He looked so scary I almost wanted to turn and run, but his voice was surprisingly high and quite kind.

I took a deep breath.

'Tia called me. She asked me to come round.'

He seemed to recognize me then, and without a word he pressed the secret button and the gates swung open. I walked past him, feeling an odd mixture of indignation and pleasure. I'd hated the way he'd looked at me at first, as if I was something the cat had been trying to bring in, but now I was in through the gates I felt special. I was one of the privileged few to be allowed inside the high walls of Paradise End.

All the way up the drive, I was expecting the front door to open and Tia to fly out, but she didn't, and when I arrived at the huge stone front step, I didn't know what to do. It wasn't like an ordinary house, where you ring on the doorbell and hear the chimes inside and know someone's there because you hear their feet coming. I couldn't even see a bell on this door, just a big brass knocker.

I was standing there, hesitating, when the door swung silently open in front of me.

'Tia,' I said eagerly, ready to run inside, but the person looking down at me wasn't Tia. It was a tall man, with brown hair cut neatly in an old-fashioned style, a long nose and an upper lip that stuck out a bit over the lower one. I know it doesn't sound like it, but he was quite hand-some, in a middle-aged kind of way.

I knew at once that it was Tia's uncle, Frost Braithwaite. His eyes were pale, not beautiful like Tia's, but nearly the same strange colour. As I looked up into them, I thought they were the saddest and coldest eyes I'd ever seen.

'You must be Tia's friend,' he said. 'How do you do.'

I wasn't sure if he was sneering at me. He was looking solemn, but the way he said it, as if I was some posh grown-up, made me feel uneasy, and when I feel like that I start getting bolshie. So I looked right back at him and stuck my chin up in the air and said, 'I'm all right, thanks. Is Tia around?'

'With Graziella, in the kitchen, I believe,' said Mr Braithwaite. 'Come into the library. You can wait for her there.'

I felt about as high as a beetle in the grass as I followed him across that huge hall, under the gallery at the back and in through a high door on the right that I'd never noticed before.

The library was long and really, really beautiful. I had to hold on to myself not to gasp. It looked like something out of one of those TV costume dramas, with books round the walls, and a great desk made of dark, polished wood, and old leather sofas and armchairs, and a huge globe in a wooden frame.

Mr Braithwaite sat down on one of the sofas. I sat opposite him on another, feeling as if the head teacher had called me into his office. Neither of us said anything for a moment, and I was starting to feel twitchy when I noticed that his left foot was bouncing up and down (he'd crossed his left leg over his right) and realized that he didn't know what to say to me either.

At last he said, 'It's Carly, isn't it?'

'Yes.'

I was sitting on the edge of the sofa, trying to look confident. There was something about him that irritated me, and I decided I'd better give as good as I got. I didn't see why he should get all the questions in, so I said, 'You're Tia's uncle, aren't you?'

He nodded. 'Yes.'

'Are you really a billionaire, like it says in the papers?'

'Yes, as a matter of fact, I am.'

I didn't know what to say then. I suppose I made a face. Anyway, a smile edged itself on to his mouth and he seemed almost human for the first time. I didn't like the way he was studying me though.

He's going to start patronizing me in a minute, I thought.

I frowned. I must have looked quite disapproving.

'I'm not used to billionaires,' I said. 'I've never met one before. I don't even know what I'm supposed to call you.'

He smiled properly, all over his face, and what he said next was really unexpected.

'Good for you, Carly. Always say what you want to say. Never pretend.'

He sounded as if he'd been trying to decide about me and that accidentally I'd said the right thing. I'd passed some kind of test. It was so dead patronizing that I was beginning to feel really offended, but then I remembered what Dad had said about Tia. 'A sitting duck for kidnappers', were the words he'd used. I suppose Tia's uncle felt he had to check me out. He didn't know a thing about me or my family. We could have been a criminal gang for all he knew, plotting to take Tia hostage and ransom her for millions of pounds. I could have been their stooge.

He wasn't the only one doing the checking though. I was taking a good look at him. If he was anything like his sister, Dixie, I reckoned Tia might need protecting from him too.

We must have looked like a couple of dummies, sitting there on those old leather sofas in that vast room, staring at each other. All of a sudden I felt I wasn't scared of him any more. He'd more or less told me to play it straight with him, and that's what I was going to do.

He seemed to come to the same conclusion about me. He pushed his long upper lip out, as if he'd made a decision, and said, 'You can call me Mr Braithwaite, if you like, but since you're Anastasia's friend, I'd rather you called me Frost.'

The word 'friend' gave me a warm feeling all the way through, and I grinned at him.

'I don't know,' I said. 'I'll play it by ear, if you don't mind.'

I knew I'd never be able to call him Frost, right out loud to his face. I decided I'd have to avoid calling him anything at all, if I could help it.

Neither of us heard Tia coming. I noticed then for the first time how quietly she moved around Paradise End. Even if she'd worn hard-soled sandals, like mine, she wouldn't have let them clatter on the wooden floors. She seemed to glide from room to room like a shadow.

One minute, only the two of us were in the room, and the next minute Tia was standing between us.

'Carly! How long have you been here?'

She was looking nervously at Frost.

'Hi, Tia.' I was relieved. Her uncle Frost was turning out to not to be too scary, after all, but I didn't know what on earth I was going to say to him next.

'Carly and I introduced ourselves,' he said.

'Sort of,' I said. 'But we haven't said much yet.'

I don't know what it was about Frost Braithwaite that made me talk so sharply. He didn't seem to mind though.

'What are you girls going to do this morning?' he said to Tia. 'Tennis? Swimming?'

I sensed Tia relax. She turned and smiled at me triumphantly.

He thinks you're great. He approves of you, she seemed to say.

'We're going up to my room,' she said. 'We've got things to do. With Graziella.'

'Is your mother up yet?' he said.

Tia's face changed, and the still look I'd noticed before came into it.

'Didn't you know?' she said. 'They never came back last night.'

His eyebrows snapped together in a frown above the high arch of his nose.

'They?'

'She went out with Otto.'

His long upper lip curled sideways.

'Otto? Otto Sanger?'

He sounded disgusted, as if he'd put his foot in something smelly on the carpet. He was about to say something else, but he stopped himself, and turned on Tia what he obviously hoped was a reassuring smile.

'They must have got held up somewhere. Don't worry, my dear. They'll be back soon, I'm sure. Now off you go. I've got some calls to make. Shall we be seeing you at lunch, Carly?'

Tia looked at me with raised eyebrows. I shrugged.

'I can stay if you want me to,' I said.

110

'Splendid,' said Frost, and he walked over to the desk and sat down in the great polished chair behind it.

Tia took my hand and pulled me out of the library. The heavy door swung silently shut behind us.

'He likes you,' she said triumphantly. 'You're so brilliant, Tia. You can never tell with Frost. He's horrible to people sometimes.'

'Yeah. Well.' I didn't want to look too pleased. 'I thought he was going to patronize me, but he didn't. I hate it when people treat me like some thick little kid.'

'Oh. Yes. I know what you mean.'

She didn't, I knew. I wanted to say, You haven't a clue what I'm talking about. You wouldn't notice if the biggest patronizer in the world patted you on the head and called you a dear little girlie. You'd smile and feel grateful, you sad idiot.

But I didn't say anything out loud. I just felt stronger inside, and protective too.

We were standing in the hall and the big front door was open. A glint of light caught my eye, and I looked out and saw that the metal gates had swung open. The silver sports car I'd seen before was driving up to the house. It turned sharply in a shower of gravel and stopped outside the front door.

Tia said, 'Oh there she is. At last.'

She started towards the door, then saw who was driving the sports car and stopped.

'Otto!' she said with a groan. 'Come on, Carly. Let's get out of the way.'

She went into the dining room. I was still looking out

at the stunning lines of the sports car, thinking of what Sam would say if he could see it too.

'Carly! In here, quick!' she hissed at me, and a second later we were both in the dining room with the door shut behind us.

'What's the matter?' I whispered.

'Otto. He's such a creep. I can't stand him. I hate it when he's here. I don't want to talk to him.'

Through one of the long windows at the rounded end of the dining room, I could see the nose of the car. Dixie had got out of the passenger seat and was walking unsteadily round the front of it. She was wearing a skimpy rose-coloured satin dress with little straps, and a necklace of big sparkling stones. Her hair was tousled and she looked creased and crumpled as if she'd been up all night.

'Come here, Otto,' she called out, slurring the words together. 'My bloody heel's broken. I can't walk on it.'

The driver of the car came into view. He was young, much younger than Dixie, and he had a mane of wavy blond hair swept back from his forehead. He was the fittest, best-looking man I had ever seen in my whole life, broad-shouldered, but with a spring like a cat in his step. I was about to turn to Tia, and ask her how she could hate such a gorgeous hunk so much, when I saw Otto bend down and pick Dixie up as easily as if she was a baby. She screamed with excitement and pleasure, like a little girl, and then I couldn't see them any more.

We could hear them though. They were in the hall now, and there were muffled noises, little shrieks and murmurs between silences, that made me feel horribly

112

embarrassed. I looked at Tia. Her lips were closed tightly together, and her cheeks were red. I thought how I would feel if someone was doing that with Mum. It was such a stupid idea it made me want to laugh, but in a revolted kind of way.

'What'll we do?' I whispered. 'We can't stay here.'

She shook her head at me.

'We can't go out *now*. Mimi'll kill me.'

We stood there squirming, not daring to look at each other, until, just when thought I couldn't bear it any longer, we heard footsteps coming down the stairs, and someone said, 'Dixie, how nice to see you. And Otto, what a pleasant surprise.'

It was Frost, and the sarcasm in his voice could have blistered the polish on the furniture out there.

I heard a gasp of surprise and confused noises.

'Frost!' Dixie gave a hiccup. 'What are you doing here? I wasn't expecting you back till this afternoon.'

'Evidently.' Frost's voice was as dry as dust.

'I'll see you then, Dix.' It must have been Otto speaking. His voice was deep, with a purr in it. It was beautiful, like velvet, but I was catching Tia's feelings off her, and beginning to hate him too.

'Otto, darling, don't go. Please.' Dixie sounded pleading, like a child, and I suddenly thought of Tia and the way she always tried to hold me back when I wanted to leave Paradise End.

'I'm sure Otto is very busy. We mustn't keep him,' Frost said, and a moment later the front door shut loudly, a car door slammed, the engine roared into life and through the window I saw the sports car drive off much too fast towards the gates, leaving deep skid marks in the gravel of the drive.

The noise of the car had drowned out whatever was happening in the hall, but as the engine sound died away, Dixie's voice changed. The slur in it had gone. It was loud and clear now, and very angry.

'I simply won't put up with this, Frost. You have absolutely no right to preach to me. I *need* Otto. He adores me. I adore him. Just because you're such a bloody cold fish yourself—'

Mr Braithwaite interrupted her. His voice was too low for us to hear what he said, but a moment later Dixie's voice, full of bitterness, cried out, 'Poor little Anastasia! That's all you ever say! What about poor little Dixie, for a change?'

I glanced at Tia. The shut look had come down over her face. She was staring up at one of the pictures on the wall, a portrait of a woman in a scarlet dress, as if she'd never clapped eyes on it before.

The murmurs went on outside, too low for us to hear.

'Where is Tia anyway?' Dixie said at last. 'She's usually hanging around somewhere down here.'

The handle of the dining-room door, which I'd thought I'd shut behind me, must have only half caught, because it suddenly clicked, and the door swung open a few inches. Tia grabbed my arm, and her fingers bit into it. I could tell she was really terrified of being discovered. Her nervousness spread to me and my heart began to race. The longer we stayed there in the dining room, listening to Frost and Dixie, the less possible it would be to open the door and go out and face them. And if they came into the dining room and found us there, it would be so awful, so humiliating, that I'd have to run away at once and never show my face near Paradise End again.

The worst was still to come though.

'Anastasia's in her room, I suppose,' Frost said, and we could hear every word clearly now. 'Her friend's here.'

'What friend? I keep telling you, she doesn't have any friends.' Dixie sound irritated.

'You mean you haven't met her?' I could practically see the disapproving frown settling on Frost's face. 'Skinny child. Spiky black hair. Says her name's Carly. Wherever did you pick her up?'

I wanted to shout, *Hey, that's me you're talking about if you don't mind.* I didn't, of course. I just stood there and listened.

'Oh her,' Dixie was saying. 'She's a friend of Margaret Marchmont's daughter.'

'I very much doubt if either Margaret Marchmont or her daughter have ever set eyes on Carly,' Frost said, his voice as dry as dust. 'Dixie, how could you be so careless? You know how vulnerable Anastasia is. She's such a little innocent. Open to all kinds of exploitation. We've talked about this. She needs protection. Security. You said you'd sort something out for her here for when Hollins is away.'

'Tia's a bloody little liar then! She told me this girl, whatever her name is, was a friend of Camilla's.' Dixie sounded helpless. 'What do you expect me to do? Check up on every whopper she feeds me? You've no idea, Frost, no idea at all, what teenage girls can be like. Secretive, sly—'

'Carly lives just down the road, on the housing estate,' Frost said, cutting across her.

'*What?* Who is she then? How on earth did she manage to wheedle her way in here?'

For two pins I'd have marched out then and there and told them both what I thought of them. I was so angry and upset I could feel myself tremble all over. Tia must have read my mind, because she caught hold of my arm again, and her eyes, looking enormous in her pale face, were begging me not to do anything.

'As it happens, it could be worse,' Frost said. 'There's nothing particularly sinister about her. I had Hollins check things out. The father's a policeman. The mother's a teacher. Not one of us, but perfectly respectable.'

'Where does Hollins get his information from?' Dixie said, sounding more curious now than angry.

'I don't ask,' said Frost. 'I pay him a small fortune to get on with it. The point is, Dixie, that Carly McQuarrie can't be a suitable friend for Anastasia. Why you haven't seen fit to provide her with better company, I really don't understand.'

'But what can I *do*?' Dixie's voice came out as a wail. 'She hates the girls at her school. She's cripplingly shy. She refuses absolutely to chum up with any of my friends' children.'

Frost cleared his throat.

'Well,' he said, as if he was losing interest in the subject. 'I suppose in the end no harm's done. I took a look at the girl myself just now.' My fists balled at the sound of the condescension in his voice. 'I rather liked her, as a matter of fact. She's a bit of a character. Might do Anastasia good.

As least she'll keep her occupied at the weekends, and the fact that her father's a policeman could be useful.'

Dixie gave a little laugh.

'Frost, you can't be serious! Tia and a policeman's daughter!'

'Then sort her social life out yourself! Really, Dixie, you are the most useless parent. You neglect Anastasia disgracefully. How can you possibly stay out all night and come home in this disgusting state, leaving her all alone?' He paused, and when he spoke again, his voice was lower. 'Don't you remember what it was like? And there were two of us.'

There was a short silence. Tia was staring at me now, her eyes so anguished I could hardly bear to look back, but somehow I couldn't look away either.

'Frost, don't be cross with me,' Dixie said, her voice like a little girl's. 'You know I can't bear it when people are cross with me.'

'Oh, go and drink some coffee and clean yourself up,' Frost said, exasperated. 'You look like a tramp. And don't go to bed yet either. I've asked Graziella to do lunch at half-past twelve. Proper lunch, in the dining room. The least you can do is pretend to look like a mother for a couple of hours, before Hollins takes the poor child back to school.'

'I suppose you want me to be charming to her ghastly little friend too.' Dixie had dropped her babyish voice and sounded resentful. 'I hope you're right about her, darling brother. Those sort of people become frightful bores if you encourage them. You can never shake them off.'

I turned away from Tia and looked out of the window

in case she saw the tears of rage that had spurted without warning into my eyes.

'Oh, I don't think you need worry about that.' I could hear that Frost was walking away from us, back towards the door of the library. 'These childhood friendships seldom last. Take my advice and let it run its course. As a matter of fact, I think we've struck lucky with Carly McQuarrie. There's something rather impressive about her.'

The library door shut. Dixie's uneven footsteps clattered away up the stairs and Tia and I were left standing in silence, in the emptiness of that huge red room.

'I'll quite understand,' Tia said in a high little voice. 'I know you'll want to go now, and you won't ever come back. I'm sorry, Carly. I'm just – terribly, terribly sorry.'

12

If Tia hadn't said she was sorry the way she did say it, I think I would have walked right out of Paradise End then and there. I was so angry and humiliated I wanted to do something horrible – vandalize the place, slash the faces in the portraits with a Stanley knife, or pick up one of the big silver candlesticks on the sideboard and smash the china parrots above the fireplace with it. But then I saw the look on Tia's face, and I knew at once just how she was feeling.

It was exactly the same as I'd felt, after that horrible teatime at home, only worse, probably, because of all the stuff Frost and Dixie had said about me.

I think it was at that very moment that Tia and I became best friends.

I don't know about you, but when I start going round with someone, nothing much happens for a while and then I realize I've got to make a decision. It's happened to me before, but it was never as important as it was with Tia. I suppose it's like that for everyone. You meet a new person, find out what they're like, and have a few laughs. You're curious and friendly, testing out what you've got in common, which bits of you are strong and which are weak, whether you can trust that person or not, and then

– bang – it's decision time. Is this person going to be my friend, my best friend, a really important person in my life? Because if so, there are things you have to be ready for, like always listening, and being loyal, and not telling secrets. It means being ready to sort things out if you disagree. Sticking by them through thick and thin. Standing up for your friend to other people.

Don't ask me why Tia and I chose each other as best friends. I mean, how different could two people be? But we did. As I said, in my mind, it fused together there and then, in that grand, red-walled dining room. Up to then, if I'm truthful, I think I'd mostly wanted to be friends with Tia so that I'd be allowed inside Paradise End. But after that it was different. I'd have been her friend wherever she'd lived.

I said, 'Weird, isn't it? Your family think I'm some horrible lowlife the cat brought in and, quite honestly, as far as my family's concerned, you could be an alien from outer space. But we're going to be best friends, aren't we?'

For the first time since I'd known Tia she looked really, truly happy. She grinned, and then the smile faded a bit and a look came into her eyes, scared but determined, a look I hadn't seen before.

'Yes!' she said. 'Yes, we are!'

We went up to Tia's room after that. It looked different to me this time. I'd felt almost like a tourist before, being allowed a glimpse of the private rooms in a stately home. Now I was in my best friend's bedroom. I belonged there.

I plonked myself down on the sofa. I badly wanted to ask Tia all kinds of things about Dixie and Frost, but I knew I had to be careful. If I let myself think too much about what they'd said about me, I'd only get angry again, and Tia would feel awful.

'Go on about your uncle then,' I said. 'Has he got any kids of his own?'

I reckoned that was neutral enough. Tia couldn't take fright at straightforward questions like that.

She shook her head.

'He was married once, but it didn't last. He was divorced ages ago. His wife went off with a nightclub owner. They didn't have any children.'

'Is that why he went all kind of cold?'

'No. He's always been like that. He must have been, or he wouldn't have got his nickname. I know this sounds horrible, but I sometimes think he's like the boy in the fairy story with a block of ice instead of a heart. He's not a bad person though. He tries to be normal. He's sweet to me, in a funny, chilly way. But I wouldn't say he was fond of me, or loves me, or anything. I don't think he can.'

I was wriggling my toes as I listened, totally fascinated.

'You know what though?' she went on. 'The weird thing is that the only person he really, truly cares about is Mimi.'

'That can't be right. He was having a proper go at her just now.'

'I know. It's like he hates her sometimes. But they're tied to each other. I can't explain it. Maybe it's a twins thing.'

'What about your mother? Does she feel the same?'

'Oh, Mimi! Honestly, Carly, I've given up trying to

understand her. I know she's my mother, and I'm supposed to love her and everything, but . . .' She looked down and started fiddling with her watch strap. 'It was different when I was little. It was OK sometimes. I can remember some nice things we did. She used to love dressing me up and showing me off. The trouble is, that's all she still wants to do. Dress me up as if I was still a baby. Sometimes I think that all I am is her designer accessory, and she can't bear the thought of me growing up. She still chooses every single thing I wear. If I say what I want, or try to do anything of my own, she puts me down. All the time. It's as if she can only see the outside of me. She's not interested in who I really am at all. You've no idea, Carly. You can't imagine how . . .'

She stopped and jumped up.

'Let's forget about them,' she said. 'It's all too depressing. Look, I've done some more work on your dress design. What do you think? Let's see if we can get Graziella to measure you up after lunch.'

Half an hour later, a rhythmic booming sound brought my head up with a jerk. Tia grinned at me.

'It's only the gong,' she said. 'Lunch is ready.'

I had butterflies in my stomach, great big, fluttering ones, as I followed her down the stairs. I'd been able to drive Dixie's words out of my head while I'd been upstairs with Tia, but now that I was actually going to face her, the things she'd said were running round in my mind like angry rats locked up in a cage.

Her ghastly little friend, Dixie had called me. *Those sort of people become frightful bores.*

How am I going to face her? I thought. What am I going to say?

The dining room looked different now that the table was set. Four places had been laid at the long table, all up at one end, two on each side, facing each other. Beautiful china plates were set out, with smaller ones at the side, and there were several glasses beside each place, and what seemed to be dozens of knives and forks.

Frost was there already, helping himself to a piece of pink fish and some vegetables from big dishes on the sideboard.

'Ah, Tia, Carly,' he said. 'Splendid. Come and have some salmon. It looks rather delicious, don't you think? No point in waiting for Dixie. She's a little tired this morning. Seems to have had rather a late night. She'll be down shortly, no doubt.'

Tia and I glanced at each other, then quickly looked away. In spite of the anger I'd felt before, I had a sudden wild desire to giggle.

I followed Tia to the sideboard (which was at least three times longer than our kitchen table at home) and helped myself to a little piece of salmon, baby new potatoes and long, thin beans. I'm not that keen on fish, actually, but I didn't dare say so. I had a sudden whiff in my nostrils of the bangers and mash that Mum always does on Sundays, and for a moment I wished I was at home, but it didn't last. I had to concentrate on what I was doing.

I sat down next to Tia, opposite Frost, and looked down at the knives and forks set out beside my plate. There seemed to be dozens of them, all in different shapes and sizes.

I knew he was watching me, and I couldn't help looking at him.

'There's an easy rule with cutlery,' he said. 'You start with the ones on the outside and work your way in.'

Thanks a lot, I thought indignantly. I can work it out for myself. To my disgust I saw that he was looking amused. I frowned back at him and he nodded, this time almost with respect. I had the same feeling I used to have watching the boys in the playground, circling round each other, not knowing if there was going to be a fight or not.

I could smell a wave of Dixie's heavy perfume even before she appeared at the door of the dining room. She'd changed into pale trousers and a linen shirt, and, except for the dark rings under her eyes, looked as if she'd been arranging flowers or something all morning.

'Darling!' she said, swooping on Tia and kissing her cheek. 'What a hopeless mother I am. Are you terribly cross with me?'

Say yes, Tia, I whispered in my head.

Tia looked at Dixie with still eyes.

'How was the director? You were going to meet a director, weren't you?'

'Oh him! You wouldn't believe it, sweetie. He didn't turn up. So rude! Luckily Otto had heard about this wonderful new club, or it would all have been too bloody for words.' She looked at me for the first time, and smiled, and her smile was so charming I could almost believe she meant it. 'It's Carly, isn't it? *So* thrilled you could come and keep my poor little girl company.'

She walked over to the sideboard and began to help herself.

'Now listen, all of you,' she said, turning back to the table. 'Otto and I have had a simply marvellous idea.'

Frost didn't even look up. He was taking a bone from his piece of salmon and laying it carefully on the edge of his plate. Tia was cutting up a bean.

'Don't you want to know what it is?' Dixie sat down beside her brother, and I saw that she had taken only two baby potatoes, three or four beans and the tiniest possible piece of salmon.

'You're all terribly slow today,' Dixie said, ignoring her food and resting her chin on her hands. Although I was wary of her, as if she'd been a bird which would peck me at any moment with its sharp beak, I couldn't help feeling a little spark of warmth every time her eyes rested on me.

The others still didn't say anything.

'Well.' Dixie gave an exasperated little sigh. 'Here's the idea. We're going to give a party! Now before you groan or say anything horrid, I don't mean a boring a little drinks party. I mean a *party*. Marquees on the lawn. A first-class band. Dancing. Lashings of champagne. What do you think, darling?'

She was looking at Tia, but Tia was looking down at her plate, cutting up a potato into tiny little pieces.

'Who are you planning to invite?' said Frost, his voice giving nothing away.

'Oh, everyone! Lots of young people, of course. All Tia's school friends, for example.'

She was smiling angelically, as if she had no idea that she was being cruel.

'I haven't got any friends at school, Mimi. You know that.'

Tia's pale little voice made Dixie frown sharply.

She's going to bully Tia now, I thought, and my fists tightened round my knife and fork.

'Surely,' Frost said, sounding disbelieving, 'you're not planning to give a teenage party.'

Dixie turned her eyes away from Tia towards him.

'Of course not! We'll invite all our friends. Lots of theatre people, and the crowd from Chieftain Studios, actors, directors – all the ones Otto and I need to meet. Guest list up to three hundred, I think.'

She suddenly turned and looked at me.

'We'll ask the Marchmonts, of course. Your friend Camilla would love to come, I'm sure.'

My heart lurched. She was playing a game with me. Cat and mouse. But I wasn't going to let her.

'I don't know Camilla Marchmont,' I said, staring back at her. 'Tia thought I did from something I said, but she got the wrong idea. She made a mistake. Tia and I met by ourselves, when her tennis ball rolled out through the gate and I picked it up and gave it back to her.'

Frost smiled.

'Well done, Carly,' he said.

I felt a shudder go through Tia. She took a deep breath, and her fork clattered nervously against the side of her plate.

'I'm not going to invite anyone from school, Mimi. I'm only going to invite Carly. She's my best friend. And she didn't say anything about Camilla. I just made that up.'

Dixie turned an astonished face towards her. No one would have blinked if I'd spoken out like that at home. They probably wouldn't even have heard me, but I realized that something amazing had happened. Tia had taken a stand against Dixie. It had taken all her courage, but she'd done it.

'Goodness,' Dixie said, with an odd little laugh. 'How very—' her eyes swept across me, sharp with dislike – 'extraordinary.'

Frost was grinning broadly.

'Have a little wine, Carly,' he said, picking up the bottle of wine from the middle of the table and offering it to me.

I shook my head. I felt as if I was in a jungle, with traps and snares all around me.

'No thanks. My dad doesn't approve of underage drinking. He's a policeman.'

I thought for a moment that Frost was going to pretend to be surprised, and play a sort of 'I know you know I know, but I'm not going to let on' game, but he just said, 'Yes, I know that. I'm afraid I asked Hollins to check you out.'

I was starting to respect Frost. At least he was being straight with me.

'A policeman!' Dixie opened her eyes wide. 'How thrilling. I wonder if he knows Sandy Shortford? He's Lord Lieutenant of the county. He has a lot to do with the police.'

She was attacking me so cleverly that if I hadn't overheard her talk to Frost earlier on, I'd probably have started feeling really small and useless. I began to realize what Tia was up against.

I mustn't show I'm angry, I thought. If I do, she'll win.

'My dad doesn't know people like that,' I said. 'He's a sergeant. He spends his time catching villains and protecting people.'

Frost burst out laughing.

'Good for you!' he said.

Dixie picked up the bottle and poured some wine into her glass. Frost frowned, and when she'd put it down he moved it away out of her reach. Dixie turned to Tia as if neither Frost nor I existed any more.

'Now, darling, we'll have to think about clothes for the party. You'll need something really heavenly to wear. *Not* the blue satin. It's all right for going out, but that colour simply doesn't work with the yellow sofas in the drawing room. We'll get you something new. We could risk black, but quite honestly you do look a tiny bit pale in black sometimes. Ricki will do your hair, of course.'

She took a long drink from her glass. Tia said nothing. She'd pushed her plate away, and was sitting with her hands on her knees, looking down at the table.

Dixie drank some more wine and turned to me again.

'And what are you going to wear, Carly?' she said, her voice thickening a little.

I stuck my chin up in the air.

'I don't even know if I'll be allowed to come. I'll have to ask Mum. She doesn't like me being out late when it's people she doesn't know.'

Frost laughed again.

'Very proper,' he said, nodding at Dixie.

Dixie shot me a glance spiked with anger and stood up. She hadn't eaten a single mouthful.

'Do you know, I think you'll have to excuse me,' she said. 'I've got the tiniest little headache coming on. Do come and say goodbye to me, Tia, darling, before Hollins takes you back to school.'

'All right, Mimi.' Tia's voice was giving nothing away. 'Lie down. Take one of your little pills.'

'Oh I will, sweetie, I will,' said Dixie, and she walked carefully out of the dining room.

'I don't get it, Tia,' I say. Lunch is over at last, thank goodness, and we've gone outside, down to the pool. Tia's lent me a bathing costume, and we're sitting on the edge, dangling our legs into the water. 'Why haven't you got any friends at school? I mean, you're a really, really nice person. I'd be your friend, if I went to your school.'

She shudders.

'You wouldn't. Not if you'd been there the first day I arrived.'

'Why? What happened?'

'Johnny drove us down. He was Mimi's boyfriend last year.'

'Last year? You haven't been there long then?'

'No. Only since September. Mimi keeps changing my school every time we move. We were in Geneva before. I quite liked it there. And before that I was in a really small school in Wales. That was OK. I had friends there. It wasn't like this place. I hate it so much, you can't imagine.'

She stopped.

'Go on. You were going to say what happened on the first day.'

Her hands are gripping the tiled edge of the pool, and her knuckles are white.

'It wasn't really Johnny's fault. He wasn't too ghastly actually, most of the time. A million miles better than Otto anyway. But Mimi was showing off, you know, about what a good mother she was. She does that sometimes. Anyway, we drove up in Johnny's car, and got out in front of what looked like the whole school, because everyone else was arriving, and Mrs Farrell, she's my housemistress, came up to say hello, and Mimi . . .' She puts her hands over her face. 'I can't bear to think about it.'

'It's OK if you don't want to tell me,' I say, moving round a bit because the sunlight's bouncing off the rippling water, straight into my eyes.

'No. I'll tell you. Anyway, Mimi was just – I mean, just so awful, you can't imagine. Terribly sweet, but deadly too. I wanted to sink down right into the ground. She insisted on being shown round the whole school. This girl, Lucia, took us, and all the others were watching, and we went to the dorm, and Mimi said, "Tia can't possibly sleep in a room without a good outlook. She simply must have a view. She's so visually sensitive. I absolutely insist that she has a room on the other side of the house." I wanted to die. Just die, you know? I could hear them all giggling behind me. And it got worse and worse. She kept saying things like, "This is ridiculous. Of course Tia must have extra French lessons. Languages are the only thing she's any good at. You're a bit of a duffer at everything else, aren't you, sweetie?" She didn't know how awful it would be for me after that. She was only trying to impress Johnny.'

Of course she knew. She must have done, I want to say.

I long to jump up and rush straight back into the house, find Dixie and strangle her with my bare hands. But Tia's sitting there too, right beside me, and she's trying not to cry, gulping in a quiet sort of way, and I know I've got to stay there and comfort her. The trouble is, I don't know what to say.

'That's so horrible,' is all I can think of. 'I'd have just – I don't know what I'd have done. Run away or punched someone or something.'

'It started the minute she'd gone,' Tia says. 'The teasing. They do it all the time. Putting stuff in my bed, pouring salt into my tea, hiding my things, calling me Dufferina. Lucia gets them all going. Everyone's scared of her. There are one or two who'd be nice, I think, but Lucia's decided to hate me and everyone else just has to go along with it.' She was twisting her hands together and the knuckles were going white. 'I just go quiet. I pretend I'm not there. I keep thinking that if I try hard enough, and go somewhere else in my head all the time, and be nothing, and nobody, I really will go away. I'll become totally invisible, and they won't be able to get at me any more.'

'I'd fight them!' I burst out. 'I'd shout and scream and beat them up! I'd put arsenic in their cornflakes and poisonous spiders in their knickers!'

She gives one last gigantic sniff and manages to smile at me.

'I know you would, Carly. That's why you're so brilliant. I wish I was like you.'

The red haze in front of my eyes is dissolving. I'm starting to think clearly again.

'You know what you ought to do? Try to make a joke of it. You know, say things like, "Hey, you guys, better be nice to me because I'm so sensitive, ha ha." Do stuff like that.'

It sounds feeble, even to me, and I can tell that it's hopeless. Tia's lost it at school. She can't win now. Dixie's messed it up for her totally and forever, and there's nothing Tia can do to put things right.

'It's Sunday!' Tia suddenly says. 'I don't want to think about school any more and ruin the rest of the day. Come on, Carly. I'll race you to the end of the pool.'

She'll win, I know she will. I'm useless at swimming. All I can do is thrash about and keep my head above water. But I jump in after her and do my best, and by the time I've got to the other end, I'm gasping for breath, and she's laughing at me. And we've forgotten about her horrible school, and we crawl out of the pool and lie down on two of the long chairs beside it to do a bit of sunbathing, and the unbelievable luxury of Paradise End closes round me again, and in spite of all the awful things in Tia's life I can feel envy sprouting up in my heart again, and I have to stamp on it hard to keep it down.

13

I can't remember all that much about the next few weeks. School was the same as usual, sometimes dead boring, sometimes quite fun. Nothing much happened at home either, except that Lauren drove me even madder than usual, pestering me all the time to remind Tia about her Barbie clothes, and Dad and Mum kept rowing with Sam, who'd started his job with Jepson's, and kept missing the last bus home to Canningtree.

The weekends had a pattern now. I'd race through my homework after school on Friday, and Tia would ring at around eight, as soon as Mr Hollins had brought her home, and we'd make our plans. I'd do tap on Saturday mornings, of course, then I'd go up to Paradise End in the afternoon, and Tia and I would mess around by the pool or bash a few tennis balls over the net on the court. Mostly, though, we'd lie around in Tia's room and talk.

Frost was hardly ever there, and Dixie was almost always out with Otto. If she was around, I'd try to keep out of her way. She was really weird with me. Sometimes she looked vague and dreamy and hardly seemed to notice I was there, and sometimes she was cruel. Once or twice she was so kind and charming that I couldn't help liking her, and wondered if I'd imagined all the horrible things.

Often, if she saw me with Tia, she'd look at me as if she'd never seen me before and say, 'Oh, it's you, Carly. You've taken my little girl away from me again. I really must be allowed a little bit of her precious weekend. Run along home, will you?'

Then, as likely as not, the phone would ring half an hour later.

'Mimi got bored and went out,' Tia would say. 'Can you come over again?'

The only thing that ever seemed to interest Dixie about Tia was her clothes. Tia might have a giant bruise on her arm from when someone at her school had tripped her up, but Dixie's eyes would slide over it, and all she'd say would be, '*Not* that yellow top with those trousers, sweetie. Do you know, I'm not sure that yellow's quite your thing after all.'

It was funny because, although Tia had enough fabulous clothes to start a boutique, she didn't care about any of them. She couldn't help looking fantastic, because everything she pulled out of the cupboards in her dressing room was super-fashionable and expensive (and perfectly ironed by Graziella, but she didn't seem to notice what she wore. The only clothes she cared about were the ones she made for her soft toys and dolls, and the dress she'd designed for me.

It was coming along brilliantly. Graziella had made a pattern for it and cut it out. Every evening, Mum said, 'I'll get sewing tonight, love, promise, after I've put my feet up for five minutes,' but every night she dozed off in front of the telly and never got round to it. In the end, Graziella said she'd rather finish the job off on her own and be done with it (I think she was afraid that Mum would mess up her work).

After that, every now and then, Graziella would come up to Tia's room when I was there, and they'd do a fitting, making me try the dress on, and taking bits in and letting bits out. I was nervous at first that it wasn't going to work. It looked awful to begin with, just bits of shiny black material hanging round me without any shape at all, but slowly I began to see what Tia and Graziella could see – the finished thing – and I knew it would be OK. It was going to be brilliant, in fact.

I'd almost forgotten about Dixie's party idea. Tia hadn't said anything about it, and I suppose I'd thought Dixie hadn't really been serious. But one Saturday morning a white envelope addressed to me appeared. Everyone (except Sam, of course) was having breakfast, and they were sitting staring at it, propped up against the cereal packet, when I came into the kitchen. I was in a rush, like I always am on a Saturday before tap.

'There's a letter for you,' said Lauren, and her little eyes were jealous and sharp and curious.

I opened the envelope and pulled out a stiff, white card. It was printed to look like old-fashioned handwriting and it said,

---

Deirdre Braithwaite
at home
Saturday 18 June at 8 p.m.

Black tie   *RSVP*
Dancing   *Paradise End*

Lauren would have snatched it out of my hand if I hadn't held it up out of her reach.

'Is it from the Wellesley?' Mum said. 'About the display?'

'No. It's a party. Tia's mum said she was going to have one,' I said, and I passed the card over to her. I wasn't sure whether I was pleased and excited or just terrified.

She read it and handed it to Dad. They looked at each other and didn't say anything.

'What does it mean, black tie?' Lauren said, peering at it over Dad's shoulder.

'Evening dress,' Mum said. 'Sounds like a posh do. Satin and diamonds. Not exactly what we're used to around here.' She curled her fingers round her coffee mug.

I suppose if I'd been listening properly I'd have realized that she wasn't exactly thrilled, but I was too stunned by the card. I took it back from Dad and stared at it again.

'I haven't got an evening dress.'

'No,' said Mum. 'You haven't. Not that it matters. I'm afraid you can't go love anyway.'

My head came up with a jerk. I thought I hadn't heard her properly. I suddenly realized that I wanted to go to the party at Paradise End more than anything I'd ever wanted to do in my whole life, except dance at the display.

'What do you mean?' I could feel panic in my chest.

'Three reasons.' Mum held up her fingers and began to tick them off in a horribly maddening way. 'One. I've been asking around at school. Carole reads all the gossip columns in the papers. She told me that Dixie Braithwaite had a terrible reputation a few years ago, going round with the wildest people. Was it booze or drugs? I can't remember. Anyway, she was in and out of rehab. It really isn't likely to be a suitable party for children. Two—'

'Right.' I cut across her. 'So I'm a child again, am I? Last night you told me that since I was nearly fourteen I should stop being childish and start taking responsibility. You are just so—'

'Two. You haven't got anything suitable to wear, and—'

'Oh haven't I? That's what you think.' Anger was building up inside me like lava inside a volcano. 'You haven't seen my tap dress. It's going to be fabulous. It's—'

'Three. That Saturday evening's the dress rehearsal for the display. You've promised Mrs Litvinov you'll be there from seven till ten. You couldn't get to the party till ten-thirty at the earliest, and even if we let you go, we certainly wouldn't let you stay after eleven. Look, love, I'm sorry, I know you're disappointed, but you'll have to send Tia's mum a polite little note saying you can't make it.'

'Routine one. Positions please,' says Mrs Litvinov, fixing her knife-sharp eyes on Lizzie, who's wriggling about, doing something to the back of her leotard. For the first time ever, I'm slow off the mark. My feet don't want to tap today. I don't really want to be here at all. I want to be at Paradise End, talking parties with Tia, planning what I'm going to wear, looking round the garden to see where the marquees will go up.

Tia looked so miserable when I said I couldn't come to the party, all slumped down and shrivelled, that I thought she'd actually got shorter. I wasn't in a sympathetic mood though, quite honestly. I suppose I was too disappointed myself.

'It'll be horrible,' she kept saying. 'I'm going to hate it. It would be different if you were there. I wouldn't be on my own.'

'On your own?' I couldn't believe my ears. 'There'll be three hundred other people, for heaven's sake.'

And, I thought, they'll all be rich and dead glamorous and there'll be film stars and celebrities – people who anyone else would kill to meet, but I didn't say a word.

Tia's mouth went into a tight, straight line and she looked stubborn for a moment, like a dog on a lead that's dug its paws in and won't budge.

'Oh, come on.' I started feeling exasperated. 'There'll be someone there you like. There's got to be someone, out of three hundred.'

She shook her head.

'Even if there was, if there was another you, or – or someone like, well, Sam or someone, I couldn't get to know them. You don't know Dixie at parties. She makes me feel, I don't know, three years old or something. She doesn't mean to, but she just destroys me.'

I could imagine what she meant. I could see Dixie grabbing all the attention, petting Tia like a baby at one moment and putting her down the next. And I could see Tia, standing on her own, being pitied and humiliated, and I stopped feeling irritated with Tia and started feeling furious with Dixie.

'Oh God, Tia, I'm so sorry. I feel I'm letting you down.'

'You can't help it. I'll manage. I'll do what I usually do, that's all.'

'What do you do then?'

'I make a plan. I work out escape routes and hiding places. I think it all out first. I'm quite good at it actually.'

I jumped up.

'They're so unreasonable! I could murder Mum and Dad for this.'

'It's not their fault. It's your dress rehearsal.'

'It's Mum and Dad too. You don't know how totally negative and stupid they are. They wouldn't let me come even if I was free. If it wasn't for them I'd skip the dress rehearsal. Pretend I had a cold or something. Say the buses weren't running. Or just bunk off. I might do it anyway.'

'You can't, Carly! Mrs Litvinov would take you off the display.'

'No she wouldn't.' I thought for a moment. 'Yes she would.' The rage roared through me again. 'I hate Mrs Litvinov! It's so mean! Why has she got to fix it for that Saturday night? It's so unfair!'

And that's what I'm feeling now, in the tap class, and that's why my feet won't work and my rhythm's all wrong, and my arms are as stiff as levers.

'Carly! What's the matter with you today? Relax those shoulders. Keep your taps clean. OK, everyone. Two more routines, and then the set pieces. From the top please, Mr Simons. Now then, shuffle–hop–step and off you go.'

There goes the piano, *tinkety-tonk*, and there don't go my feet.

'Carly!' Mrs Litvinov holds up her hand and Mr Simons stops playing. 'What are you doing? Sea-lion

139

impersonations? On the fourth bar it goes tap, tap, shuffle–hop–step and flap. You know that. We've done it dozens of times. Again please, Mr Simons.'

I get through the class somehow, all stiff and clumsy, like a doll. Mrs Litvinov stops going on at me after a while, but I can feel her sharp black eyes on me. For the first time ever I want her to leave me alone. I don't even respect her any more.

At the end of the class she calls me over.

'Right, Carly. What's the problem? You were all over the place today.'

'Sorry, Mrs Litvinov.'

'Sorry isn't good enough. Sorry isn't going to get you through the display.'

I don't say anything.

'Well, come on. Don't just stand there. Something's bothering you, I can tell.'

She's looking almost sympathetic and a flicker of hope lights up my heart. If I ask her really nicely, if I explain, maybe she'll change the date of the dress rehearsal, or even let me off. I take a deep breath.

'It's next Saturday,' I say. 'I've got a problem with the dress rehearsal.'

'Yes?' I can see concern in her eyes. She's expecting me to say something kind of emotional, like it's going to be my nan's funeral that day, or I've got to visit my brother in prison. I can hardly say, *There's this amazing party that I've been invited to, and it's in a stately home with marquees and a band and loads of incredibly famous people.* Now can I? I can't even think up a false excuse fast enough.

All I manage to say is, 'My best friend needs me that night, Mrs Litvinov. She's got a problem with her mum. She really, really needs me.' And that's the truth after all.

Mrs Litvinov bites her bottom lip. She's shaking her head. I know I'm on to a loser. I don't know why I even gave it a try.

'I'm sorry, Carly, but a dress rehearsal's a dress rehearsal. If you want to be in the display, you have to be there. You've made a commitment and now it's time to honour it.'

On she goes, and I'm not even listening. I could have said it all for her anyway. I'm concentrating on holding my temper back. Then I realize she's asked me a question.

'Your costume,' she says again. 'I asked you to bring it today. Where is it?'

'I haven't got it. It's not finished.'

I know I sound sulky, but I can't help it.

She frowns again.

'Today was the last day. I warned you last week.'

'I know, but . . .'

She's looking at me as if she's wondering if she made the right decision, and I have a horrible feeling, down in the pit of my stomach, that she's going to bump me off the display. That sets me into a right old fright.

'Honestly, Mrs Litvinov, it is nearly ready. And it's lovely. Fantastic. Wait till you see it.'

'I am waiting, Carly.'

'You'll love it, I know you will. My best friend designed it. She—'

'What?' She's looking worried now. 'Your best friend? How old is she?'

141

'Fourteen, but she's brilliant. It—'

'Carly, I do hope you realize that the way you look is vitally important. I haven't imposed a uniform on you, only specified black and white, but . . .'

'I'll have it at the dress rehearsal,' I say, nodding frantically at her like a total freak. 'I promise. I'm picking it up this afternoon.'

She heaves a sigh.

'I suppose it'll have to do. There'll be a few more days if we need to make adustments. In the meantime, Carly, you must work on your attitude. Tap comes from the heart as much as the feet. I'm sorry about your friend, but you've got priorities here and the display should be up there at the top of your list, with nothing else on your mind.'

I can see Lauren at the door, mopping all this up, and I can't wait to get away.

'Yes, Mrs Litvinov, sorry Mrs Litvinov,' I gabble. 'Got to go or I'll miss my bus,' and I dash out of the room, grab Lauren's elbow and yank her after me, desperate to get out of there.

I know I've gone on a bit about my dress, but you should have seen it, especially that afternoon when I tried it on, finished, for the first time, in front of the long mirror in Tia's dressing room.

I couldn't see it properly at first, because Graziella was fussing round, twitching at the collar and peering at the hem, but at last she stood back and said, 'Yes, is OK now. What you think, Carly?'

What did I think? I was too dazzled to think anything much, except that I looked about twenty-five years old,

142

and dreamily cool, and not all bones and angles for once, but fluid and floating.

I did a quick tap routine, even though it didn't make a sound at all on the carpet.

'It's – oh, I can't say,' I said at last. 'Fantastic. Brilliant. Everything.'

'It'll look OK with your tap shoes, won't it?' said Tia, looking down at my feet. 'Look, Graziella. There's a pin still stuck in the sleeve.'

I felt uncomfortable. For a moment Tia had sounded really grand, like someone talking to a servant.

'The shoes'll be fine,' I said. 'You two have no idea. I'm just so impressed. I wouldn't have believed – honestly – I look . . .'

It's not often I'm lost for words, but I was that time. Then a nasty thought struck me.

'My hair lets it all down. Story of my life. I'm going to shave it off and get a wig.'

Tia laughed.

'Carly, you're a complete idiot about your hair. It's great. Unlike anyone else's. Totally your own.'

'Totally my own sad, revolting mess you mean. Thanks a lot.'

She was shaking her own honey-blonde hair at me.

'People spend years looking for a style. You've got one. It's terribly easy to look like me – blonde bimbo – so obvious. We're everywhere.' She hesitated. 'That's what I want to do, if ever I get to be a real designer. Not make loads of fashionable clothes, like everyone else does, but help people find the way they want to look. You know, make them feel better about themselves. So that they can bring out the person they really want to be.'

At least, I think that's what she said, but by then I wasn't listening. I was too busy admiring my dress in the mirror.

'There's only one thing I really hate,' I said.

'What?' Tia looked anxious all of a sudden.

'That I'll be wearing this to the display and not to your party.'

'Oh, the party.' Tia's face had cleared, but it clouded over again. 'I was trying not to think about that.'

Graziella undid the zip at the back of the dress and I climbed out of it again.

'Don' be silly, Tia,' she said, sounding bored, as if she'd said the same thing hundreds of times before. 'Is a nice party. Lots of kids your age.'

Tia made a face at me behind her back.

'OK, you two,' Graziella went on, 'I got to go now. The wine is coming this afternoon. Big delivery.'

She'd been holding the dress and now she laid it down on the back of a chair.

'Graziella, I just, I mean, thank you so much,' I said. 'You've no idea. It was so lovely of you to do it.'

She smiled as if she was surprised.

'No problem, Carly. I like to sew. Is good to keep in practice.'

'I can't get over her making this for me,' I said, stroking the rich, black silk as Graziella left the room.

Tia shrugged.

'Why? It's all part of her job.'

The uncomfortable feeling came back and I felt a stab of resentment.

144

'No, it isn't. She did it like a favour. It was really, really nice of her. She probably did it for you anyway, not for me, just because she's fond of you.'

'Oh, fond!' Tia raised her eyebrows.

'Yes. You heard me. Fond.'

Tia looked uncomfortable. She walked away from me, out of the dressing room and into her bedroom where she stood in the middle of her acres of carpet, maddeningly distant and aloof. I followed her. I wasn't going to let her slip away. I wanted to sort this out.

I felt suddenly as if she was looking down at me from somewhere high above. It annoyed me.

'You don't understand, Carly,' she said.

'I don't, as a matter of fact. I don't believe in treating people like they're inferior, or slaves or something. Just then, when you told Graziella to take the pin out of my sleeve, you sounded like a flaming duchess. In fact, you sounded exactly like your mum.'

Tia flushed.

'Maybe I am like her. She's my mother, isn't she?'

'No! You're not like her at all! She's heartless. She never thinks about anyone except herself.'

Tia didn't say anything. The red flush was deepening in her cheeks.

'Oh God, I'm sorry.' I jumped on to the sofa and began banging my forehead down on a cushion. 'She's your mother. It was an awful thing to say about your mother. It was just the way you spoke to Graziella. I couldn't believe it. I mean, she's a really nice person, and she cares about you. I know she does. And you . . .'

'I told you, Carly, you don't understand.' She was

frowning as if she was looking for a way to explain, but couldn't find the right words.

She sat down beside me and began running a finger round a button on her top. I made myself go quiet and still, to encourage her to talk.

'What don't I understand?'

'I'm Graziella's job. Don't you see that? She's paid to look after me. OK, she likes showing me how to sew. We don't mind spending time together, but next year, when she's saved enough money, she's going back to Italy. She's going to open a dress shop in her village. She talks about it all the time. Do you really think, once she's gone, that she'll ever give me another thought?'

'OK, but that doesn't mean—'

'When I was little, there was Lizzie,' Tia went on, as if she hadn't heard me. 'I really, really loved her. She used to put me to bed. Sometimes I sat on her knee, and she bounced me up and down. She even read me stories when she wasn't too busy.'

'There you are, you see? You were her job too, but she loved you and you loved her back.'

'Did she? She couldn't be bothered to stay with me. She left when we moved to Geneva and someone offered her more money. She used to send me postcards sometimes, but she doesn't any more. After her there was Martine. I hated her. She pinched me when I cried. Mimi sacked her after a bit because she was rude about Perry – he was Mimi's boyfriend then. I can't remember all the others. There was one called Birgitte who I really liked, but she left, and then Cathy, and Imelda and Beata. None of them ever stayed for long. Mimi always quarrelled with them

146

and gave them the sack.' She shook her hair back and looked at me, and her eyes were bleak and defensive at the same time. 'In the end you just begin – well, what's the point? You have to protect yourself, because in the end everyone leaves.'

There she was, sitting beside me on that luxurious sofa, dressed in her beautiful clothes, shaking her long, shining hair back from her shoulders, when, I don't know why, a picture came into my head. It was like something from a children's book, a story of a princess who was building a wall round herself, brick by brick, imprisoning herself in a tower. Making a shell. A place to hide.

Maybe that's what Dixie did, I thought. Maybe she was like Tia once: a nice person, but she grew a kind of armour for protection, and the real person died inside and all that was left was a shell.

'No!' I said loudly, making us both jump.

Tia looked quite scared. I could see she was afraid I'd turned against her.

'I'm not going to let you do it!' I said, thumping my fist down on the arm of the sofa.

'Do what?'

'Build a wall round yourself. Close up. Stop being able to love and trust people.'

She looked puzzled.

'I haven't. I don't.'

'No, but you might. You've got to get one thing into your head anyway.' I took a deep breath. 'You can trust me. You can count on me. I'm not going to go away and stop sending you postcards. You can't give me the sack. We're best friends now and you're stuck with me for life.'

I suppose I'd expected her to look pleased and say something about being my best friend forever too, the way anyone else would have done. She did start to smile, a really hopeful, nice smile that started in her eyes, but then she looked away again.

'I know you mean it, Carly,' she said. 'It's awfully sweet of you.' She hesitated and looked embarrassed. 'But you can't help being so busy. I don't blame you at all. I mean, you've got your family and your school friends and your tap and everything. You haven't even got time to come to the party.'

I felt my heart lurch, as if it had decided what I was going to do even before my head had. Up to then, I'd wanted to go to the party just because it was grand and exciting. Now I suddenly saw that it was a test, the first test of our friendship. If I wanted Tia to stop building up the bricks of her tower, I was going to have to take the biggest risk of my life and get myself into all kinds of trouble.

'Well you're wrong then,' I said. 'I am coming to the party. I'm going to bunk off the dress rehearsal and come up here instead, and no one's going to stop me.'

14

I'm not usually devious. I tend to go for things head on. 'Like a bull at a gate,' Mum says. But I could see, as I walked home from Paradise End that evening, with my beautiful dress carefully packed in a carrier bag in my hand, that I was going to have to be cunning if I was to get to the party without my whole life falling round my head in ruins.

The thought of it filled me with a mixture of excitement and dread. I didn't even try to think about the display, and what Mrs Litvinov would do when I didn't turn up to the dress rehearsal.

I'll get round it all somehow, I kept telling myself. I'll think of a way. I'll call her and tell her I'm ill or something. It'll be all right.

But I didn't think it would be. Mrs Litvinov's got eyes like X-rays. She can see right through excuses and read your mind. I've seen her do it to people dozens of times.

It was the usual Saturday evening at home. Lauren was slumped on the sofa, watching TV. Mum was sitting at her desk in the corner, marking piles of exercise books. Dad had just come in off duty. Normally, I'd have burst in and shown everyone my new dress, put it on and pranced about in it, but the thought of what I was planning to do was making me feel peculiar.

'Hello, love,' Mum said, looking up. 'Had a good time?'

I could see she wanted to be nice to me. She thought I'd be in a mood about missing the party, and she was trying to be sympathetic.

'I've got my dress. It's finished,' I said, not looking at her.

'Good,' said Mum. 'Did you say a proper thank you to Graziella?'

'No. I told her it was rubbish and asked her to do it all over again. What do you take me for, Mum?'

'Let's see,' said Lauren, rolling over and trying to grab the bag out of my hand.

I jerked it out of reach.

'Watch out! You'll mess it up.'

She lost interest and went back to the telly.

Dad put his head round the door.

'Where's Sam?'

'Out working,' said Mum. 'Jepson's are catering for a private party over at the Crown ballroom. He said it might be a late do.'

'It isn't,' said Lauren. 'He gets off at nine. I heard them tell him on the phone. He's trying to get Ellie Smithers to go clubbing with him afterwards.'

The smug look on her face made me feel sick.

'You're a slimy little snake, Lauren,' I said, making a hideous face at her. 'You have absolutely no regard for other people's personal space.'

Mum frowned at me, but didn't say anything. Dad had gone upstairs.

I heard the front door open and shut again, and Sam came into the sitting room.

'You're early,' Mum said mildly.

'Stood you up, did she?' Lauren said, looking pleased.

Sam threw a cushion at her, but his eyes were on me. He looked half wary, half excited, as though he was gearing himself up for a fight.

'How was the do?' Mum said. 'Did they run you off your feet?'

'It was OK. Someone got pissed and we had to chuck him out. I spilt some wine down my white jacket. Can you wash it, Mum? I'm going to need it again next Saturday.'

He was still looking at me.

Mum put a final tick in the last exercise book, closed it and dumped it down on the pile. She stretched her arms out and yawned.

'Oh yes?' she said. 'Jepson's have got another party on, have they? What do they want you to do this time? Washing up or waitering?'

'Waitering,' Sam said, and paused.

'Where is it?' said Mum. 'Not too far away I hope. I always worry in case you can't get yourself home.'

A horrible feeling was crawling through me. I knew what Sam was going to say before he even said it.

'Couldn't be nearer.' He was backing towards the door. 'It's the party at Paradise End. The food and the caterers are coming down from London, but Jepson's are doing the serving.'

Mum's and Lauren's heads swivelled round to look at me. I knew they were expecting me to go mad, blow up like a firework and scream and yell. But I just felt a cold

151

hand of worry clutching at my insides. Things were complicated enough without Sam being involved.

I couldn't think of a thing to say. I pushed past him, went up to my bedroom and slammed the door shut.

The only place I wanted to be next morning was Paradise End. I had this burning secret inside me, and I knew that if I stayed at home, I wouldn't be able to help blurting it out.

What with sleeping a bit late though, and being made by Mum to tidy up and do some homework, it was gone twelve o'clock when I finally arrived at the big front door.

'I don't want any lunch or anything,' I said to Tia, who had opened the door to me herself.

I couldn't face the thought of another tense meal in that gloomy dining room, with Dixie playing cat and mouse with me.

'It's all right,' Tia said, reading my mind. 'It isn't a proper lunch. It's so hot today we're having something outside by the pool. Frost isn't here anyway. He doesn't get back from Zurich till tonight.'

I followed her upstairs to her bedroom.

'We're trying things on for the party,' Tia said over her shoulder. 'Come and help choose.'

'Who's "we"?'

'Mimi and me.'

My heart sank. Being with Dixie was like being in the same room with a wild creature, all fur and feathers at one moment, and all teeth and claws the next.

But it was obvious, as soon as I went into Tia's dressing room, that Dixie was in a good mood. She was sitting on the stool in front of Tia's dressing table, a vague smile on her face.

'Carly,' she said. 'We need you. You can tell us what you think. After all, what does an old fogey like me know about what girls wear these days?'

She looked funny and sweet and helpless, and I couldn't stop myself smiling at her.

'Don't be silly, Mimi. You're not an old fogey,' Tia said automatically, as if she'd been given a cue and was producing the right lines. 'You're frightfully elegant. You know you are.'

'Darling, you're so sweet,' said Dixie. She pointed at the cream-coloured dress, which was hanging from the hook on the back of the door. 'Try that one on again. You've got to choose, sweetie. It's that one or the pink one. You know what I think. The pink. Think the pink.' She seemed to be having problems getting her words out.

As usual, her perfume filled the room with its heavy scent, but as I walked past her towards a little basket-work chair in the corner, I caught an unmistakable whiff of something else. Alcohol.

I sat down in the chair and looked at Dixie. She was balancing carefully on the stool, trying to focus her eyes on Tia, and then I understood. Dixie was drunk. Out of it. Off her face. Wrecked. In the middle of the day.

The weird thing was that Tia didn't seem to notice. She was looking with anxious loathing at the coral-coloured dress hanging over her wardrobe door.

'Mimi, please, no,' she was saying. 'I *can't* wear that thing. It makes me look like a marshmallow.'

'All right, my pet. No need to fuss.' Her voice was sugary, as if she was talking to a child. 'We'll send the howwid pink one back to Stefano. If Tia wants the cweam one, she shall have it. Put it on again. Let Carly see it.'

Tia shot a look at me. The expression in her eyes was long-suffering and apologetic. She threw off the top and shorts she was wearing and began to scramble into the cream dress.

Dixie wasn't looking. She was staring at herself in the triple mirror on Tia's dressing table. She moved her eyes for a moment to look at Tia's reflection behind her own, then went back to staring at herself.

'Nice. What do you think, Carly? Isn't she pretty?'

The dress was utterly gorgeous. It fell round Tia in soft folds almost down to the floor. It was held up over the shoulders by little straps that sparkled with a frosting of tiny diamond-like stones.

'It's fantastic,' I said, feeling envious of Tia and nervous of Dixie at the same time. 'You look great, Tia.'

Tia stood squinting down at herself. Dixie dragged her eyes away from the mirror at last and turned round.

'Pretty but boring,' she said, and I couldn't tell if she meant Tia or the dress. 'Needs cheering up a bit. Diamonds cheer things up. I'll let you wear my bracelet, darling. It's full of diamonds. Dozens of diamonds.'

'Thanks, Mimi,' said Tia in a colourless voice. She was trying to undo the zip. I helped her. The dress dropped to her feet in a silken whisper.

'Pretty,' said Dixie again, looking at her daughter as she stood there in her bra and pants. 'Darling Tia, so pretty.'

Tia looked at her warily, like someone who's been given a present to unwrap, but is afraid there's something nasty inside. Then she dived for her top and dragged it on.

Dixie's face fell and she heaved a huge sigh. For an awful moment I thought she was going to cry.

'Proud of you,' she said. 'I'm a bad mother. Useless. No good. Can't be a good mother. Not me.'

Tia was in the act of pulling on her skirt as Dixie said this. She stopped for a moment, as if her mother's words had paralysed her.

Dixie tried to stand up, and had to sit down, but she made it on the second attempt.

'Got to go,' she said.

I couldn't watch her as she staggered out of the room. I felt – what did I feel? Embarrassed, I suppose, and scared, in a way, but more than anything else horribly, horribly sorry for Tia.

Why hasn't she said anything to me? I thought. She can't not know. Her mother's a total alcoholic. What am I going to say?

I didn't need to say anything. I looked up and saw that Tia was watching me.

'She isn't – it's not usually this bad,' she said in a small voice, and if I'd been embarrassed she looked a million times more so. 'She gets like this sometimes, for a month or two, and then she stops and doesn't touch a drop for ages. It's Otto who's making her so unhappy. When she gets like this about someone, obsessed, I mean, she just can't think about – about anyone else.' She swallowed. 'Look,' she went on, recovering and speaking more normally, 'do you mind if we don't talk about it any more? I

155

usually try not to notice. There's nothing I can do anyway.'

'No I don't mind.' I felt relieved. 'I'm only sorry for you. It must be – I mean – doesn't your uncle . . .'

I stopped. I was pushing her too hard. She shrugged, and I could tell she wanted to change the subject.

'Never mind about Mimi,' she said. 'It's been worrying me, what I said yesterday, about you not having time to come to the party. It was so mean of me. It was like I was forcing you to say you'd come. I did, I suppose, because I wanted you to so badly, but I'm scared you'll get into trouble at home, and you'll be thrown out of the display, and anyway, you'll hate the party, because you won't know anyone except me, and Mimi will be horrid to you and . . .'

She looked miserable and confused. I felt a steely resolve forming inside me.

'I'm coming,' I said. 'I said I would and I am. It's all settled. I'm not backing out now.'

15

The worst thing about the next few days – the really *awful* thing, in fact – was that everyone (except Lauren of course) was so nice to me. Mum went on and on about the display, telling me how proud of me she was going to be, and Dad started shifting over to the middle of the sofa when we were all watching TV, so that I could sit in the comfy corner. Even Sam stopped teasing me.

Mum kept saying things like, 'I know you're disappointed about the party, love, but honestly, you probably wouldn't enjoy it. You wouldn't know a soul there apart from Tia, and if the newspapers are right about the sort of people Dixie Braithwaite hangs out with, you probably wouldn't want to know them anyway.'

The worst moment was when she said, 'Carly, I'm impressed. You've taken your disappointment better than I'd expected. Get yourself a cup of tea and let's have a chat and a biscuit before you have to get started on your home-work.'

'Can't Mum. Haven't got time. Sorry,' I said, diving for the door.

She'd have been stunned and furious and upset if she'd known what I was planning to do, and the thought made me feel so guilty I couldn't bear to be in the same room with her. My mind kept spinning round and round, churning up my feelings like a giant paddle. One moment I was determined to go to the party and stand by Tia whatever happened, and the next moment I was so terrified at the thought of bunking off the dress rehearsal and facing the most awful row at home I'd ever be likely to have in my whole life that my legs would hardly hold me up.

Mum'll never speak to me again, I thought. Dad'll kill me. Mrs Litvinov'll cast me off. My dance career will be over before it's begun.

But deep down I didn't waver. I was going to get to the party whatever it cost.

I still hadn't got a clue about how I was going to manage it. I'd have to be sneaky about it, of course. I'd have to pretend I was setting off for the dress rehearsal, but slip off to the party instead. Later, when it was all over, I'd just have to face up to everyone's rage and fury.

I was beginning to hope, though, that Mrs Litvinov wouldn't have to know the truth. If I could think up a really good reason why I hadn't turned up, she'd have to accept it and keep me in the display. I lay awake every night, trying to work it out, and my plans got wilder and wilder.

I'll phone Mrs Litvinov last thing Saturday afternoon and tell her I've been struck down with a lightning dose of summer flu, I thought, as I tossed and turned in my hot little bed.

No, she'll phone back before the display to find out if I'm better, and talk to Mum, and that'll be that.

I'll say there was a bus strike and I spent the whole evening trying to get into Torminster, but gave up in the end and had to go home.

That's useless. Everyone'll know that's not true.

How about if I say I was on my way to the dress rehearsal, and a gang of lads took me hostage, and I didn't manage to escape till ten o'clock, when it was all over?

Grow up, Carly. She'd tell you to go to the police and report it. She wouldn't buy it in the first place anyway.

In the end, I decided that I'd just have to wait till the last minute, and hope that inspiration would strike.

The last class at Wellesley before the display was on the morning of the party and the dress rehearsal. For the first time ever, I didn't want to go. I found I was dragging my feet down to the bus stop, with the carrier bag with my dress in it bumping against my thigh. I didn't know how I was going to look Mrs Litvinov in the eye.

I knew I had to face her though. For one thing, I had to show her my dress (I was quite looking forward to that bit actually), and for another, I was nervous about my dance. I needed, badly, to practise it in front of her one last time.

'Pity your dress rehearsal's this evening, isn't it?' said Lauren, as we stood waiting for the Torminster bus. 'Shame you've got to miss Tia's party.'

That might sound OK to you, as you read it on the page, but trust me, it wasn't. There was triumph and curiosity and a horrible pleasure in her eyes. I gave her a look back that would have scorched a hole right through anyone less thick-skinned than Lauren. I'll say this for her though. She's got a good sense of self-preservation. She shut up then and there and I didn't hear another squeak out of her all morning.

As soon as we got to the Wellesley Centre I ran up to the cloakroom and put my dress on, then went to show it off to Mrs Litvinov. Her eyes widened when she saw it.

'Very, very nice, Carly. It's elegant and exactly right for your routine. Did your friend really design it? A talented girl, obviously.' She hesitated. 'I'm sorry you've got to let her down this evening, but that's life, isn't it? Things always seem to clash. Anyway, commitment has its own rewards. I don't often say this to students, but I don't mind telling you. You have a rare talent for dance, and talent always involves sacrifice. Get out of that lovely dress now and put your leotard on. We've got work to do.'

If she'd said all that, about me being talented, any other time, I'd have floated right up into the air till I'd bumped my head against the ceiling. As it was, I just felt numb with guilt.

'Right,' she said, when the class was lined up in the hall. 'We're going to do our warm-ups first, then work through our normal routines, to relax you. Those of you taking part in the display will go through the set pieces one by one. We won't overdo it this morning, because you'll be running through it all again tonight at the town hall. Over there, though, we'll be concentrating on getting you used to an unfamiliar stage, and the effect of the lighting, so this is your last chance for a real practice.'

I felt hollow inside when she said that. The way I'd thought about the dress rehearsal, it had just been something boring that I'd wanted to miss. Now I realized that I needed it. Next Wednesday night, when the display began, I'd have to step out on to a strange stage in front of a whole battery of lights, and seats that were full of strangers. I would have missed my chance to get used to it. I wouldn't know what the hell I was doing. My heart lurched with fright.

It was an effort getting through the morning. I had to drive everything out of my head and concentrate on the dance. Every time I relaxed, a battle started up in my mind.

Stuff the party. You can't possibly miss the dress rehearsal. You need it.

No. I promised. I told Tia I'd go to the party. I'm not going to let her down.

'Carly! You missed the beat there. Do it again. Once more please, Mr Simons.'

I got through somehow, and dragged a silent Lauren home with me.

No one was surprised when I went upstairs that afternoon and slammed shut the bedroom door. I suppose they expected me to be in a mood. I could hear the house slowly emptying. Sam went off somewhere with his mates. Dad was cutting the grass in the back garden. Lauren had skipped off to the swings with Darren and Francine. I couldn't hear Mum. Sometimes she nods off on the sofa on a Saturday afternoon.

I lay on my bed and thought about things. Now that the morning and the actual presence of Mrs Litvinov was fading a bit into the distance, and the evening was getting closer, I was beginning to feel a bit less worried and a bit more excited. So what if I was going to land myself in one hell of a row? In a few hours' time I'd be wearing the most beautiful dress I'd ever owned, and I'd be swanning

161

around in Paradise End at the most amazing party I would ever be invited to in the whole of the rest of my life.

I sat up. I had things to do. Wash my hair, for one thing. I went to the door, ready to go to the bathroom, then paused. Mum was coming up the stairs. She must have decided to lie down on her bed instead of on the sofa. I waited until I heard her door shut, then opened mine.

What happened next was so amazingly lucky that afterwards I took it to be a sign. If the phone had rung twenty seconds earlier, Mum would have picked it up downstairs. If it had rung twenty seconds later, I'd have been in the bathroom with the shower turned on and I wouldn't have heard it at all. As it was, the minute it rang I ran downstairs and picked up the receiver.

'Hello?' a man's voice said. 'Is that Carly . . . er . . .' He paused, as if he was reading from a list. 'McQuarrie?'

He sounded so strange I nearly said, 'Is this a dirty phone call? Because if it is you're out of luck, mate, and anyway a policeman lives here, so bog off.'

But I didn't, thank God.

He cleared his throat.

'This is Daniel Litvinov. My wife Pat's your tap-dance teacher, I believe.'

My first thought was that Mrs Litvinov had read my mind. She knew I was about to bunk off the dress rehearsal, and she'd called in her husband to get heavy with me.

'Yes,' I said cautiously.

'She asked me to call.' His voice was a bit unsteady. 'I'm afraid tonight's dress rehearsal at the town hall's been called off. Pat's mother's been taken very bad. She's had to rush her over to the cardiac unit in Durstow. She told me to ring round and tell everyone that she'll try to fix something up before the display, on Monday or Tuesday.'

'Oh!' I said. 'Oh. Thanks for telling me, Mr Litvinov. I'm really sorry about Mrs Litvinov's . . .'

But he'd put the phone down already.

I put the receiver back and stood there, while the glorious realization of what he'd said flooded through me. I knew I ought to feel sorry about Mrs Litvinov's mother, but I couldn't. A mountainous weight had rolled off my back, and a big warm, rosy sun had risen in my mind. I wasn't going to have to make up silly lies to Mrs Litvinov. I wasn't going to have to let her down and see disappointment in her face. I was going to go to the party *and* get my badly needed rehearsal after all.

I suppose I ought to have run upstairs right then and told Mum at once, and got her to agree to let me go to Paradise End that evening, but I didn't. She was so down on the whole thing. I knew she'd get into a state and put her foot down, and ask Dad to come in and back her up. And if they did let me go, they'd make Sam promise to keep an eye on me, and they'd tell me I had to come home practically before the party had started.

No, I couldn't tell Mum. Anyway, as the timing had worked out so brilliantly, it looked as if I was *meant* to go to the party. It was something I was *supposed* to do.

I looked at my watch. It was only half-past two. There were hours and hours before I could start getting ready.

The house felt small and enclosed all of a sudden, shutting me in. I looked round for a pencil and some paper.

'Gone for a walk. C.', I wrote, and left it on the kitchen table. Then I went out and shut the door quietly behind me.

Why didn't I go up to Paradise End and try to see Tia? I don't know. I did walk up to the gates and look through them, glimpsing the corner of a huge blue-and-white-striped marquee that had been put up on the lawn below the terrace, and seeing men carrying around tables and little spindly-legged gold chairs. I knew Tia would come running if I pressed the buzzer by the gate and asked for her, but for some reason I wanted to be on my own.

I turned down to the left, and walked past the long blank wall of Paradise End's grounds towards the main street of the village. It was oppressively hot and sticky, and the sky was hazing over as if a storm was on the way. I wanted to go the cool way, down under the trees by the canal, but I was doing enough deceitful things for one day and I'd promised Mum I'd never go there on my own.

I walked the long way round, behind the main street and out the far end, at the edge of the village, where the old church was. Beyond it the fields stretched away into the distance. There was a side gate into the graveyard. Big trees hung over the mossy old stones, and the shade underneath them looked cool and inviting.

I slipped in through the gate. I didn't want anyone to see me. They'd think I was being weird, all by myself on a Saturday afternoon, mooning around in a churchyard.

There was a bench under the trees. I sat down on it and curled my legs up under me.

I can't remember all the strange thoughts that went

164

through my head that hot summer afternoon. I suppose I was feeling nervous and excited and guilty, but it was more than that. It was as if I was standing on the brink of something, as if I was about to go through a door, and that I'd soon be leaving the old Carly behind and stepping out as a new person.

Everything about that shady green place is as real to me now, thinking about it ages later, when so much else has happened, as it was at the moment when I was sitting there. I can practically hear the faint rustle of leaves overhead as a slight breeze stirred them, and smell a heavy, damp, woody smell from the boggy corner of the nearby field. I can see the hazy sunlight glowing on the graves, and the rooftops of the old part of Canningtree, which stretched away from me up the hill towards the gates of Paradise End. The new part of the village, the network of streets like ours, was out of sight from here. It seemd as if it didn't exist any more, as if my home and family had never been, and I was alone in an eternal place, somewhere in the past, or in the future, it hardly mattered which.

I am who I am, I thought. I might even be an everlasting soul. I know where I begin and other things end.

Perhaps it sounds odd, but that's what I thought, that afternoon.

I must have sat there for ages, quite still, just being. It was the bee that woke me out of my trance. I'd heard it for a while at the edge of my mind, buzzing round a cluster of honeysuckle flowers in the hedge behind me, and then it started coming in close, and made me move along the bench.

I looked at my watch and yelped with surprise. It was nearly half-past four, and I'd have to pretend to leave for the bus stop on my way into Torminster at half-past six. Before that I had to wash my hair, sort out my shoes, decide if I was going to wear my white beads, put some make-up on and fuss and panic in front of the mirror.

I slipped off the bench and ran home.

16

You know how it is sometimes with luck? You can get runs of it, good or bad. I was dead lucky that afternoon. For one thing, no one was in the bathroom. No one was standing outside the door either, banging on it, while I gave myself a good long shower and washed my hair.

The next good thing was that Lauren had stayed out with her horrible little friends, and I had the bedroom to myself. I could concentrate on my hair, and for once it turned out to be not too bad – better than the usual hedgehog look I manage to end up with anyway.

I heard Sam come in and rush around, hunting for his waiter's gear, but my luck still held because a little later the front door banged shut behind him. I was really glad I wouldn't have to face him before the party. It would be bad enough bumping into him, as I was sure to do, up at Paradise End.

I tried my dress on again and spent ages looking in the mirror, trying to see myself from the side and back view. I know I'm not anything much to look at, so don't think I'm being vain when I say that there was something special about me that evening. It was mostly the dress, I suppose, the perfect swirl of black satin, the hint of 1920s glamour,

167

the fall and the cut of it. But it was in me too. There was something new about me, a clearness and togetherness. I don't know how to describe it. Just believe me when I say I'd never looked like that, never looked so good, before.

There'll be loads of boys there, I told myself, with a shiver of excitement. Really cool ones. Not like the no-hopers at school.

At half-past six Mum shouted up the stairs, 'Your tea's ready, Carly. Come and eat before you go.'

That gave me a shock. I wasn't one bit hungry. In fact, my stomach was churning round like a washing machine. Anyway, I knew there was going to be the most amazing five-star buffet up at Paradise End, and I wanted to have room for it. Most of all, though, I didn't want to sit in the kitchen face to face with Mum, putting up with her being nice to me.

'What is it?' I yelled.

'Pizza. Your favourite. Ham and pineapple.'

Quickly I slipped the dress off and laid it down on my bed.

'Sorry, Mum,' I called out, 'I've got to go. Wrap it up for me. I'll eat it on the way.'

'Got to go?'

I could hear her footsteps on the stairs, and I was into my ordinary clothes faster than greased lightning. I was just doing up the zip on my jeans when she appeared at the door.

'Why do you want to go so early? The bus doesn't leave till seven-fifteen.'

'Said I'd meet Lizzie,' I mumbled, turning away from her. 'Don't stop me, Mum. I'm late already.'

She came towards me and I was afraid she'd give me a hug. I dodged out of her way. I didn't want her to see the make-up on my eyes.

'Have you got a carrier for your dress?'

'Yes, of course I have.'

'You know the last bus goes from the town hall in Torminster at ten-fifteen? Mrs Litvinov promised you'd be out in time to catch it.'

'I know.'

'Got your bus money?'

'Yes!'

I knew I sounded irritated, but I was desperate for her to go. At last she did.

'OK, love. I'll get your pizza ready.'

There was no point in waiting any longer. I was as ready as I'd ever be. It was much too early for the party, but I'd need time to change when I got there. It would be dead embarrassing, arriving at the gates in my awful old clothes, but I'd just have to slip up to Tia's room and get dressed up there.

I folded my dress carefully and put it into the carrier, along with my best strappy shoes and my white beads. I ran down the stairs. Mum had the pizza ready. She was looking at me, a little worried frown cutting into her fore-head. I couldn't wait to get away. I grabbed the warm pizza in its foil wrapping out of her hands and turned towards the door.

'Got your tap shoes?' she called after me as I ran to the front door.

My heart jolted.

'No! Wow! I nearly forgot.'

169

I raced upstairs, grabbed the shoes and belted down again, then I was out through the front door and away.

I'd worked out what to do. I didn't turn right, towards Paradise End, in case Mum was watching me out of the sitting-room window, but ran off to the left, towards the bus stop. I planned to turn right along the main road, down to the bottom of the village and work my way round by the lane that led up the side wall of Paradise End, back towards the big gates at the top of the hill.

I was halfway down the main street when I caught sight of myself in a shop window. I stopped dead and stared. The elegant me of twenty minutes ago had gone. Wearing my old jeans and T-shirt I looked like I always did, but worse somehow, like a stupid, scruffy kid. Up at Paradise End, Tia would by now be getting ready to put on her stunning cream dress. Frost would be in a dinner jacket with a black bow tie. Dixie would be wearing God knows what fabulous creation, and dripping with jewels too, if she wasn't too drunk to put them on.

I felt panic sweep over me. I'd been crazy to want to go to this party. Mum and Dad had been right. I'd be a fish out of water, a square peg in a round hole, a fly in the ointment.

I haven't got a present to take, I thought, another wave of fright almost knocking me out. I don't even know if you are supposed to take presents to a party like this.

I caught the reflection of a woman walking along the pavement behind me, and saw that she'd turned her head and was looking at me looking at myself. I felt my face go scarlet, and hurried on.

Then, down at the bottom of the hill, I caught sight of the stones of the old church, and an idea came to me. I'd go back to the shady place under the trees. I'd be all alone there. I could slip out of my jeans and T-shirt and put on my dress, and I could wait for a while, until nearer eight o'clock. It would be much easier, walking up that grand drive, if I looked OK and I wasn't horribly early.

The sun had got lower and had moved right round while I'd been at home. The old bench wasn't in the shade now, and even though it was getting late it would still be too hot to sit there.

I went round to the far side of the churchyard and sat down on a pile of stones by the wall, under the branches of an overhanging tree. I needed to cool off a bit. The tension and heat of the last hour had started to undo all the good of my shower.

I looked round. No one was there. It would be easy to change here without anyone seeing me.

Then I heard voices coming down the lane. I moved right back against the wall and waited.

The churchyard gate creaked as it opened and two women came in. One of them was carrying flowers. They walked away from me, down to a row of newly dug graves near the bench. I relaxed a bit. I could tell they hadn't seen me.

The women stopped by one of the graves. The older one took a bunch of dead flowers out of the vase by the headstone and emptied out the water. Then she filled the vase again from a bottle and arranged the fresh flowers in it.

It sounds funny, I know, but until that moment I hadn't thought of the churchyard as a cemetery. It had just seemed like a nice quiet place, a place to think and feel apart, where you could be yourself. But now the low sun was sending dark shadows from the lines of tall old gravestones across the grass, and it felt different, full of sadness and endings and thoughts of other worlds.

The women stepped away from the grave and moved back along the path towards the gate. They still hadn't seen me.

'Too hot for me, this weather,' the younger one said, wiping her forehead.

The other one looked up at the sky.

'Yes. It's gone sultry. There'll be a storm tonight, I shouldn't wonder.'

Did I shiver at that moment? Did I have a premonition of what was going to happen. I don't think I did.

The churchyard gate squeaked again as it shut behind them.

I felt out of place. I was about to go to a party. I was going to dance and eat fabulous food, and be beautiful in a stunning dress, and have the most amazing fun with my best friend. I was going to look cool and sophisticated and keep my end up and show the world that Carly McQuarrie could hold her own with the best of them, however posh they thought they were.

'What on earth am I doing,' I heard myself say out loud, 'lurking around in this spooky old graveyard, for heaven's sake?'

I hid behind the biggest tombstone, took off my jeans and T-shirt and zipped myself into my dress. I clasped the

172

beads round my neck and slipped my smart shoes on to my feet. Then I bundled my old clothes into the carrier bag. The scruffy me had gone. The elegant me had magically returned.

At that moment, I heard music wafting down from the great house above, and the sound of car doors slamming. The party was starting.

With my heart pounding in my chest, I walked out of the churchyard, up the hill, towards Paradise End.

17

By the time I got to the gates of Paradise End, cars were arriving – Porsches and Jaguars and Alfa Romeos – and people were stepping out of them, the men in black or white dinner jackets and the women in dresses like ones you only see in magazines.

I stood there hesitating, looking in round the left pillar of the gates. I hardly recognized the house. There was a striped canopy over the front door and a red carpet running halfway down the gravel drive, with little trees in flowerpots on each side of it. There were people everywhere, guests in their fabulous clothes, chauffeurs in grey caps, waiters in short white jackets.

Then I heard a familiar voice.

'That's right, sir. Drive round to the left behind the garage. There's parking on the other side of the house on the north lawn.'

It was Mr Hollins. He waved the car on and turned round and saw me. For once, his heavy face split open in a smile.

'Wotcha, Carly. Tia's been waiting for you. Come on in.'

'Where is she?'

'Up there. She's been on the lookout for hours. Where've you been?'

He pointed up to the house. I moved round past the gate pillar and looked up. I could see the whole front of the house now, and there in an upstairs window was a slim, pale shape that moved and disappeared. A couple of seconds later, Tia came out from under the canopy and ran down the drive towards me.

'Carly! You came!'

She was looking at me as if she couldn't believe her eyes.

'Course I came. I said I would, didn't I?'

'Get out of it, you two. You're blocking the traffic,' said Mr Hollins, shooing us away from the gate to let a huge white Rolls-Royce come gliding through them.

Tia led me away from the drive down on to the lawn below the terrace, where the marquee was standing. She slipped behind a clump of bushes, and I followed her.

'This is one of my hiding places,' she said, 'that I'd planned to use if you didn't come. But you did. I just can't tell you, Carly . . .' She broke off and looked down at my dress. 'It's OK, isn't it, the dress I mean. It does work. Actually, I think you look rather stunning. Those beads are exactly the right thing, and I really like the way you've done your hair.'

My confidence was beginning to climb back up again.

'You look brilliant too,' I said.

She shook her head, the way she always did when I said something nice about her looks, as if she was tossing the compliment away.

'I can't believe you've done this for me, Carly. Giving up the dress rehearsal and everything. You've got no idea what it means to me.'

175

'Well, as a matter of fact . . .'

I was about to tell her about Mrs Litvinov's mum, and how Mr Litvinov had called me, but the shining look in her eyes stopped me. I didn't want her to think I'd only come because the dress rehearsal had been cancelled. It would have spoilt it for her.

The band in the marquee had been playing all this time, ordinary background stuff, but now it revved up to a real dance number. And then I felt it. A blaze of excitement and a fierce joy surged through me. After Frost and Dixie, Tia was the most important person at this party. And I was Tia's best friend. I was at the centre of it all. I had a *right* to be here.

'Come on,' I said. 'What are we doing, hiding in here? Let's go to the party!'

I take Tia's hand and we come out from the bushes and walk across the grass. People are arriving in a steady stream, parking their cars down the hill to the left of the house, moving round to the far side on to the terrace and drifting down the wide stone steps from the terrace towards the marquee. There are all ages here, some quite old, lots of people like Frost and Dixie, but younger ones too, around twenty or twenty-five, and quite a few our age as well. There's a group of them standing around on the terrace, laughing nervously.

I walk right up to them, with Tia coming along shyly behind me. The excitement's pounding through my veins, propelling me along, but it's tinged with nerves now. If this crowd give me hassle, my confidence will fizzle out and I'll come to a dead stop like a car that's run out of petrol.

176

'Hi,' I say. 'I'm Carly.'

Two of the girls look at me as if I was something wriggling out of a muddy pond, then they giggle. They turn to Tia.

'Wow, Tia,' one gushes in a super-grand accent, 'what a fabulous dress.'

'Thanks, Camilla. So's yours. Fantastic,' Tia says, sounding posher than I'd ever heard her sound before.

I take a good look at Camilla. I feel I know her already. And I don't much like what I see. Her nose is wrinkled and her top lip's curled up as if she can smell something nasty. I guess she usually looks like this, but I can't help thinking she's searching for a way to put me down.

My bubbles start to run out, like Coke that's going flat. I don't belong here. I'm a fly that's landed on a big cream cake and any minute now someone's going to swat me off it.

Then I look up and catch the eye of one of the boys. He's grinning at me. He's got a really nice face, with a squashy nose, and his hair sticks up like mine does.

'Want a drink, Carly?' he says. His voice is a bit posh too, but not sneering like Camilla's, and he looks cute as he pulls at his black bow tie to let a bit of air get to his neck. 'Don't tell me you're not dying of thirst. It's practically tropical tonight. What do you want? Champagne?'

'Brilliant,' I say.

He waves at a waiter, who's passing along the terrace with a tray in his hands, and my heart misses a beat. What if it's Sam?

It isn't, thank God.

The boy picks up two glasses of the pale, bubbly wine

and hands one to me. The boy next to him, who's shorter and looks shy, hands one to Tia. The others help themselves.

'Cheers,' everyone says, and the boy with the squashy nose raises his glass towards Tia and me.

'Rory,' Camilla says to him, flashing me a sideways look, 'are you going to the point-to-point on Sunday?'

'Not sure.' Rory's still looking from Tia to me and back to Tia again.

'What about you, Tia?' says Camilla. 'Oh, sorry. I forgot. You don't like horses, do you?'

I feel Tia stiffen up beside me, but she doesn't say anything, and the others all start talking about horses. Tia and I are standing there like a couple of losers, out of it. I take a sip of champagne. I've never had it before, and I can't say I like it much. It's sour. But it starts to fizzle through my veins straight away.

Then I sense someone coming up behind me, and I turn round. Frost is here. He's wearing a white dinner jacket and unlike everyone else he doesn't look too hot. He's taller than ever and grand and lordly.

Uh-oh, I think. Here we go. Now for some cutting down to size, and I have to stop myself hiding my champagne glass behind my back.

But he gives me a friendly smile and, what's better, he ignores all the others.

He says, 'Hello, Carly.'

I say, 'Hiya, Frost.'

It's taken a surge of courage to call him by his nickname, and I'm scared for a moment, but he just says, 'How nice to see you. Delighted you could make it. I

178

gather you had to cut a rather vital rehearsal to get here.'

I shrug and say, 'Not a problem.'

'I hope you approve of the band,' he says, looking around at all of us. 'I'm not sure what you young people like dancing to these days. It's all just noise to me, I'm afraid.'

'It's great, Mr Braithwaite,' says Camilla in a smarmy, breathy voice.

'Well, enjoy yourselves,' he says vaguely and walks off.

The atmosphere's changed. Camilla's dropped her sneer and everyone looks at me with respect.

'Are you a frightfully famous actress or something?' says the short boy who'd given Tia her champagne. He sounds impressed.

'No, she's a frightfully famous dancer,' says Tia, and I'm scared in case she goes off into one of her flights of fancy and sets me up for a fall, but luckily, before she gets going, Camilla gives a shriek.

'Oh!' she squeals. 'There's Petra! I haven't seen her for *ages*.' And she runs off down the lawn, and the other girls follow her.

Dixie appears out of nowhere. She smiles at me, but the smile doesn't reach her eyes. They move past me and fix on Tia.

'There you are, darling. I was afraid you'd run off and hidden somewhere. *Such* a little shrinking violet.' She gives Rory and the other boy a blinding smile. 'Now why aren't you all dancing?'

And she drifts off, her pale-green silk dress rippling round her body as she goes.

'Shrinking violet?' I say, shooting sideways looks at the boys to make sure they're listening. 'Tia? That's all she knows.'

The boys laugh, and look at Tia with more interest. I can see they think she's gorgeous. She clocks it too. She's blushing a bit, and tossing back her hair.

'Rory! James!' yells Camilla. 'Come and talk to Petra. She says you always ignore her.'

Rory rolls his eyes.

'Don't go away, you two,' he says. 'We'll be right back.'

He leaps off down the terrace steps towards the group of girls, and James, with a last admiring look at Tia, goes after him.

'They both fancy you like mad,' I say to Tia.

She giggles.

'No they don't. It's you.'

'They like us both then,' I say, 'because we're cool and fascinating and totally irresistible.'

I don't know whether it's that sip of champagne or the look in the boys' eyes, but something's gone whizzing to my head.

'Come on,' I say, grabbing Tia's arm. 'Let's go and see what's happening. Let's check this whole party out.'

She hangs back.

'But those two. Rory and James . . .'

I stare at her.

'You're not going to wait around for them, are you? Let them come and find us. Make them sweat a bit. It never fails.'

*

180

Oh, it was fairyland at Paradise End that night, and we were like two winged spirits, Tia and me, flitting about everywhere, filled with laughter, slipping from room to room, she in her pale dress and me in my dark one.

The light was going now. Mr Hollins had lit the drive all the way from the gates to the front canopy with flaring torches, and the flames sent unearthly shadows dancing into the house.

We started in the drawing room, sliding into it through the long French windows from the terrace. The huge room gleamed soft and gold, a treasure house of beauty. I thought no one was there, and I wanted to throw out my arms and shout out loud, but then we heard a sound and we turned round and saw a man in a white jacket and a woman in a scarlet dress kissing each other on one of the sofas at the far end. Mad laughter burst from us both. The couple looked round, but by that time we were out of the far door, tiptoeing across the hall.

No one was in the dining room. I looked up and caught the stern eye of crazy old Joshua Braithwaite, staring down at me out of his portrait, with his factories behind him. The walls glowed a deeper red than usual, and I had the oddest feeling that they were really made of rose petals and would be soft if I touched them.

'Tia, look, the colours are all different tonight,' I began, but she had gone out again, and I ran after her, back across the hall and into the library, where two solemn men were standing with their backs to the empty grate, holding their champagne glasses against their bright-white shirt fronts.

'Do you think the press have got hold of it yet?' we heard one of them say, and for some reason it made us laugh even more, and we sidled past them, out of the library, into the conservatory beyond, holding ourselves in till we could collapse into a pair of cane chairs beneath the fronds of a huge fern.

But the conservatory was airless and stiflingly hot, and we were filled with wildness and happiness and strength. We couldn't stay still, so we were up again a moment later, bursting out through the glass doors, right beside the swimming pool. The water was so beautiful with the lights of the great house sparkling on it, and it looked so cool and welcoming that I could have thrown myself into it then and there. I stood poised on the edge, almost ready to dive, then I turned and looked at Tia, standing there too, and we read each others' minds and shook our heads and laughed a bit more.

Something had changed between us. I'd been ahead before, with Tia behind me, but now she had taken the lead, and I was following her. And we went on through the rose garden, round the sundial, through the trellis and out past the cherry trees, and then we came to the far end of the terrace where the buffet was laid out.

I stopped and stared, my mouth open, because never in my life had I seen such food: turkeys and ducks, lobsters and hams, yellow rice and bowls of salad, tomatoes carved like flowers and pineapples carved like trees. There were swans made of ice holding butter in hollows in their backs, and sauces, and different kinds of rolls, and another table groaning with sweets – strawberries, cakes, meringues, tarts and mousses – and everything was so beautiful, so tempting, that my mouth watered hard and I had to swallow.

'Look at this, Tia,' I said. 'Look at all that.'

But her eyes had swept over it indifferently as if it was nothing special to her. She was looking down to the other end of the terrace, and I saw that Rory and James had seen us, and they were pushing past people on their way towards us. Someone else, an older person, came up and started talking to Tia, and she turned away to answer.

Then I had a heart-stopping shock, because standing right in front of me, a tray of glasses in his hands, was my brother, Sam.

'Carly!' he gasped. 'What on earth are you doing here? What about your dress rehearsal?'

I pushed one shoulder out towards him, getting myself geared up into fighting mode.

'It was cancelled. And before you ask, Mum and Dad don't know. They don't know I'm here either.'

I could see he didn't know what to think. He couldn't decide whether to play the disapproving big brother or admit to himself that he admired my guts.

'You'll catch it,' he said at last.

'Don't think I haven't worked that out.'

I grinned at him, and to my relief, he grinned back.

'It'll be worth it anyway,' I said. 'Isn't this the most amazing thing you've ever been to in your whole life? I wouldn't have missed it for anything.'

He pulled a face.

'All right for some. Lousy rotten hard work for us. I'm dripping with sweat and my feet are killing me. They're going mad in the kitchen. They took a risk, putting the buffet outside. It'll all be wrecked if the storm breaks. I think it will soon. Can't you feel it in the air?'

We looked up at the sky. I hadn't noticed before, but even in the near darkness we could see that black clouds were rolling up over the horizon towards us, blotting out the last glow from the summer night sky.

'I've got to go,' Sam said. 'Look, Carly, watch out for yourself. This isn't a kids' party. Don't go mad or anything.'

'Yes, and you bog off with your tray and stop cheeking the guests,' I said, but he hadn't stopped to listen.

I looked round. Rory and James seemed to have got stuck halfway along the terrace. Tia was still talking politely to the same person. At last she turned back to me.

'Were you asking that waiter for a drink?' she said. 'Is he going to bring something? I'm terribly thirsty.'

'No.' I hesitated. I hadn't told Tia about Sam being there. I suppose I'd felt ashamed, of my brother being here only as a waiter, and I'd half hoped we wouldn't run into him. But there was no help for it now. 'It wasn't a waiter. Well, it was too. It was Sam. My brother. He's got a job with the firm that's doing the catering. I'd have told you, only – I didn't get round to it.'

'What? *Sam?*' Her head whipped round and she stood on tiptoe to look over the crowd at his disappearing back. 'Why didn't you say anything? Is he coming back this way? That's so amazing, I . . .'

She didn't finish, because Rory and James came back, and they said did we want to go down to the marquee, where the dancing was, and we said yes, and we all went down together. The band was great, a bit old-fashioned and not loud enough for me, but OK, and we danced for ages.

It was strange dancing with older people. They were doing really weird things, like out of the eighties, but we got into it after a bit, and got going with the rhythm and just ignored them all.

A couple of times I saw Camilla looking into the marquee, scowling when she saw us, and once I saw Dixie flinging herself across the dance floor with Otto, but mostly I was only aware of the four of us, Rory and James laughing and sweating and trying to keep up with me, and Tia, who'd jumped right out of her cool, sleek self for once, and was shimmering around in her gleaming dress, her hair flying, a smile of pure happiness on her face.

Then the band stopped playing, and people started appearing with plates of food in their hands, so we pushed our way up to the buffet and helped ourselves. We sat on the terrace steps and ate the most delicious things I'd ever tasted in my life, and I felt for the first time that I was beautiful and clever and sophisticated and cool, and I wanted to stay there forever, to be there forever, in the heat of that magical night, sitting on the sun-warmed stones with my best friend, while the boys teased us and admired us and made us feel good.

The first drop of rain fell as I put the last frosted strawberry into my mouth. It splattered down on to my plate, the size of a fifty-pence piece. Another one fell on my knee, and another on the top of my head. We all jumped up. Some people were running down the terrace steps, back into the marquee. Others were moving quickly into the drawing room through the French windows.

'Come on,' said Rory, pulling me to my feet. 'Let's go inside.'

There was such a crowd trying to push across the terrace that I had to let go of Rory's hand. I found myself up against a pair of broad male backs, right in front of me. One of the men was Otto. The other was an older person with a mass of thick, white hair. They were moving forwards slowly, as if they hadn't noticed that at any moment the rain would start pelting down.

I was just about to push between them, when the older man put his arm up and patted Otto on the back, completely blocking my way. I heard him say, in a strong American accent, 'You know what, Otto? You sure as hell got lucky tonight. You're looking at it straight in the face. Your break. The big one. A part to die for. Fall in love with fame, baby. It's coming your way.'

Otto turned, and I caught a glimpse of his face. He was biting his lip, holding back the huge grin that was trying to split it in half.

A space opened up beside them, so I could have stepped round them and gone inside, but I was too interested. I wanted to hear more.

Otto mumbled something.

'Oh, Dixie!' laughed the older man. 'We love dear Dixie, of course.' He made a bunch with his fingers, kissed the tips, then spread his hand out to blow the kiss away. 'But my dear, so yesterday. And that legendary temper! The alcoholic breath! Take my tip. Cut loose. She's served her turn. You can do better than Dixie.'

Otto laughed, and I could hear relief in his voice.

'Oh, I will. I will. It'll be no sacrifice, believe me.' He gave an exaggerated shudder. 'Have you ever seen her in a full screaming tantrum? Or even worse, when she's trying to be cute?'

The older man laughed too.

'Frankly, I don't know how you have put up with her for so long.'

'Frankly,' said Otto, 'neither do I.'

I suddenly realized that Tia was standing just behind me, listening to every word. I saw her face, but I couldn't bear to go on looking, and screwed my eyes shut.

'Otto!' came Dixie's voice from the far end of the terrace.

'Time to quit, I think,' said Otto. He turned back, and ran quickly off down the terrace steps.

Dixie ran up to us.

'Wasn't Otto here? Where did he go?'

She sounded strained, almost desperate. Her hair had lost its perfection. It was straggling round her face, which suddenly looked old and haggard.

'Who cares where he went, Mimi,' said Tia, and I'd never heard her speak so like an ordinary daughter to Dixie before. 'He's a pain. Let him go. Please.'

'Not now, sweetie,' Dixie said, as if Tia was a child who'd begged for an unsuitable treat. 'Otto!'

She looked wildly round, saw Otto disappear from the bottom of the terrace, then plunged down the steps and stumbled after him across the lawn.

The raindrops had been coming thicker and faster, and now the first flash of lightning zipped across the sky. Tia and I dashed across the last few metres of the terrace towards the drawing-room windows, but in the lightning's sudden dazzling brightness I caught sight of Frost, and let Tia go on alone.

Frost was standing quite still on the edge of the terrace, alone, not seeming to notice the rain, looking down to where his sister was chasing Otto across the grass below.

18

The party changed. Before, the people who hadn't been dancing in the marquee had been spread out in the grounds, lingering in the rose garden or talking and laughing on the terrace, but they'd crowded into the house now. They were filling the drawing room, spilling out into the hall and even into the dining room beyond.

Dixie seemed to have given up pursuing Otto. She was standing on the stairs, a glass in her hand. She was waving at a second band, a jazz quartet, who had been playing all evening on the gallery.

'Turn up the sound!' I think I heard her shout. 'Dim the lights!'

Someone did, and the music pounded out. The table had been cleared away, and the hall had become a dance floor. People were moving in and out from the open rooms dancing more and more wildly.

It should have been great, like being in a fantastic club or something, but I'd started to feel uneasy. Tia had disappeared again and there was no sign of the boys. I looked for them, but couldn't see anyone I knew. The faces of the people looked strange in the dimmed light, no longer happy and partyish, but desperate and strained.

Where's Tia? I thought, anxiety crisping me up inside. Is she all right?

Then I heard the smash of breaking china and looked back into the drawing room. Through the open door, I saw that one of the pair of huge old Chinese vases on the mantelpiece had disappeared. A woman near to where it had been was shrieking in a voice full of panic, 'There are snakes on the other one too!' I saw a trembling hand covered with rings pick the second vase up and drop it. There was another smash as it broke on the floor.

She must be having a fit or something, I thought. I wish I could find Tia. What's the matter with me? I'm getting freaked out here.

Just then a tray loaded with glasses of wine seemed to appear out of nowhere, and I snatched one off it. But before I could drink, a hand grabbed my wrist, holding it painfully hard, and half the wine tipped out down the front of my lovely dress.

'What the hell, Carly. You were drinking champagne before. You've had enough.'

It was Sam.

My anxiety flipped into a flash of fury. I wrenched my arm away.

'Get stuffed, Sam. Leave me alone.'

'Carly, I'm telling you. Watch out. You need to stay on top of things, OK?'

'I told you,' I snarled at him. 'Get lost.'

Usually, Sam sparks back at me when I rip up at him, but this time he didn't. He just stood there looking at me, his forehead ruckled up with worry.

'I mean it,' he said. 'Be careful.'

190

'What are you on about?'

His serious look had calmed me right down.

'There's all sorts going on here. Heavy stuff. God knows what. You shouldn't be here, Carly. I think you ought to go home. It's gone half-eleven. Mum and Dad'll be going spare by now.'

All my life, I've refused to let Sam boss me around, but for once I wanted to cave in. He looked strong and steady, standing there, a proper big brother, and I was beginning to feel out of my depth.

But I shook my head.

'Can't. I can't just go and leave Tia.'

'Where is she?'

'That's the trouble. I don't know. I lost her when we came indoors. I'm worried about her.'

We'd been shouting to make ourselves heard above the music, but it stopped suddenly. I could hear the rumble of thunder and the noise of torrential rain pounding on the ground outside.

'I can't go home anyway,' I said. 'Not till the rain stops.'

'Phone Mum then,' said Sam. 'Tell her you're OK.'

He was right. I knew it. My heart was sinking faster than a pebble in a pond.

'I had to come, Sam,' I said, trying not to sound pleading. 'Tia really needs me. I've got to find her.'

He actually nodded.

'Yeah. I can see that. I'll back you up with Mum. Look, I've got to go.'

He disappeared into the crowd as the music started up again. I fought my way through to the stairs, ran up a few,

191

and looked down over everyone's heads, but I couldn't see Tia, or the boys for that matter.

Phone Mum, I told myself. You've got to do it. Get it over with.

I'd only ever phoned from Paradise End using Tia's mobile, but I remembered the desk in the library. There'd been a phone on it, I was sure. And the library would probably be quieter. Somehow, I couldn't imagine people raving away in there.

I shoved my way through to the back of the hall again, and opened the library door.

I was right. It was quiet in here, almost empty, in fact, but not quite. Tia and Otto were there.

I'd never seen Tia being angry before, but I could tell she was furious now. Her cheeks were bright pink. Her arms were straight and stiff and her fists were clenched. In a controlled, tight voice she was saying, 'You've lived off my mother for months and months. You've taken everything she's given you. She did this whole party for you. How could you have said those awful things?'

Otto ran his fingers through his hair. He was trying to look cool and charming. I couldn't imagine how I'd ever thought he was gorgeous. His face was slimed over with the most disgusting insincerity.

'Look, Tia, you're a sweet kid,' he said, 'but you've got to – well, face facts. People do say things. I said things. I'm sorry you overheard. I didn't know you were listening. I didn't mean to be nasty about your mother. It's time for me to move on, that's all.'

If I'd been Tia I'd have clawed his face. I could see, though, that her contempt was much more effective than

192

rage. Otto was looking uncomfortable. His eyes were sliding sideways as if he was trying to work out how to get past Tia and the big desk and out through the library door.

'Next time you decide to use somebody, and then just dump them –' Tia began, but she never finished, because the door burst open and Dixie came into the room.

'Otto, darling!' Her voice was thick. I'd gone over to stand beside Tia, but she didn't notice us. She stumbled across towards Otto and tried to put her arms round him.

'I've just heard! Isn't it brilliant? Such a wonderful part for you. Max is too divine. Hollywood, here we come!'

Otto unwrapped her arms from round his neck and stepped away from her.

'Look, you kids, can't you leave us for a bit?' he said, shooting us a sideways glance.

'Oh, are you here, Tia, darling?' Dixie waved unsteadily at Tia. 'Isn't it wonderful? Back into the big time.'

Otto's eyes narrowed.

'Max hasn't – has Max offered you . . . Who told you about my part?'

'Lally, of course. I haven't seen Max yet. He must be hunting for me everywhere.'

'Mimi,' Tia began, 'listen, it's not going to be . . .'

But Otto was suddenly between us, taking us each by an arm and thrusting us towards the library door.

'Out,' he said. 'Now.'

The door slammed behind us.

'I knew it, I knew what he was like,' Tia said. 'The snake.'

I was hopping up and down.

'Snake? He's a rat! A skunk! A dirty piece of lowlife!'

'Shh.' Tia put a hand on my arm. She bent her head against the door, trying to hear what was going on inside, but the noise of the band and the laughter and shrieks of the guests in the hall drowned out everything else.

We stood there for a while, not knowing what to do. Then I saw Sam on the far side of the hall, balancing a tray on one hand above his head.

'Mum! I never called her!' I mouthed to Tia in a panic. 'Where's your mobile?'

She pointed to the stairs with her chin.

'Up there. Come on.'

We were about to start pushing our way through the crowd when the library door burst open. Otto was trying to push Dixie back, but she was clinging to his arm. Then he lost his temper completely.

'Get lost, you old drunk. I can't stand all this any longer,' he shouted.

He freed himself at last, and sent Dixie spinning against the door frame. One or two people standing near us had heard, and they turned shocked faces to Otto, clearing the way in front of him as he lunged through the crowd towards the front door.

Things happened quickly after that, horribly fast, but I can see it all still, quite clearly in my mind. Dixie recovered her balance and tried to follow him, shrieking, 'Otto! Come back! Don't leave me!'

The desperation in her voice made more heads turn. She didn't notice. She reached the front door. Tia had tried to catch hold of her arm, but Dixie was outside

194

already, running in the rain, down the red carpet with its little border of trees.

There came a roar as Otto started his car, then we saw the rear lights glow red as it swung out through the gates of Paradise End and disappeared down the hill.

Dixie faltered and swayed in the driveway for a moment, then she plunged towards her own scarlet sports car.

'No, Mimi! No! You can't!' shouted Tia, running out towards her.

A kind of paralysis, a creeping horror, held me back. The band in the gallery were still playing, their cheerful rhythm pounding on, but no one was dancing now. People were crowding out through the front door to stand under the canopy, or pushing to a window to get a better view.

For a moment, the scarlet sports car didn't move. The lights from the flaming torches, still fizzing in spite of the torrential rain, glittered on its polished sides. I could see Dixie fumbling behind the steering wheel, and Tia trying to wrench open the door by the driving seat.

'Mimi, you can't! Come back!' she was shouting.

But the engine roared into life. The car leaped forwards, lurching violently, making straight for one of the pillars of the gates, then swerved at the last minute and shot through them. People were shaking their heads and muttering anxiously, but no one spoke loudly, and the music hadn't started again.

I found my feet at last, and raced out to meet Tia, who was running back towards the house. The rain had darkened her long blonde hair, which was hanging now in rat's tails over her shoulders, and her dress was nearly wet through. I dragged her into the shelter of the canopy.

'Frost! We've got to find Frost!' she said. 'Someone's got to go after her!'

'Mr Hollins,' I said.

Her face brightened.

'Hollins, yes. He'll know what to do.'

She darted out again into the streaming rain, towards the garages. I took a deep breath, ready to follow her.

'What's going on?' said someone behind me.

I turned and saw Sam.

'Dixie. She—'

'I know. I saw. Where's Tia?'

'Trying to find Mr Hollins. She wants him to go after her.'

He nodded. 'Good.'

For the first time in my life, I saw that Sam looked like Dad, steady and solid. I nearly wanted to fling my arms round him.

'Sam, I still haven't been able to phone Mum,' I said.

He tapped the mobile he kept strapped to his belt.

'I have. Good thing too. She was going nuts. She was just about to get Dad to pull in the entire British police force.'

My heart sank right down into my toes.

'Is she totally, totally furious?'

'Dunno. Yeah, at first. I told her you had to be here for Tia. Said you'd be staying the night. She calmed down.'

'You calmed Mum down?' I was awestruck. For once in my life, I didn't know what to say.

196

Suddenly, Tia was back.

'Was he there?' I said.

'No.' She was pale and shivering, wet from head to toe. 'What'll I do? What am I going to do?'

'I'll find him,' said Sam. 'Don't worry. Go inside and get warm.'

He pushed Tia gently back in through the front door and ran outside again.

Up on the gallery, the band was still playing, but only a few couples were dancing, circling around dreamily, their energy gone. I could tell that the party was more or less over. People were fetching coats and wraps, looking round uncertainly for someone to say goodbye to, ducking their heads as they prepared to dash out to their cars through the rain.

Tia was trembling so violently that I could almost hear her teeth chattering.

'You ought to change. You need to get dry,' I said, more roughly than I'd intended. I took her arm and tried to pull her towards the stairs.

'No!' She pulled away from me. 'I've got to find Frost!'

Her anxiety was starting to claw at me too. I kept imagining Dixie, who'd hardly been able to stand upright, behind the wheel of a fast sports car. It would be swerving violently all over the road, turning corners too fast, skidding on the wet surface.

'You're right,' I said. 'We've got to find Frost.'

The nearest open door was the drawing room's. It was a mess, as if a tidal wave had washed over it, the chairs pushed around, red gashes of wine staining the sofas, half-empty plates of food littering the tables, the fragments of the Chinese vases lying in the grate.

One quick look told us that Frost wasn't there. Tia had already moved on towards the library. I followed her, and looking in through the door, I saw Frost, sitting at his desk, quite still, his back straight and his arms crossed on his chest.

'Frost! I can't find Hollins! He's got to go after her!' burst out Tia.

He turned his head stiffly towards her.

'He's gone. I sent him almost at once.'

Tia's knees buckled. She sank down on to one of the leather sofas.

'Oh, thank goodness. He'll know what to do. He's sure to stop her. She'll be OK, won't she, Frost?'

It was almost as if he had seen her for the first time.

'Yes, of course. Tia, look at you! You're wet through. Go and change. I'll let you know as soon as she comes back.'

Tia smiled. I could feel her relief. A weight was rolling off me too.

Out in the hall, the music had stopped and the band were packing away their things. The last few guests were standing about talking, or looking out through the windows as if they were waiting for the rain to stop. They moved aside as we walked through, and I saw pitying looks on some of the women's faces. Tia didn't notice them. She was shivering again, but only with cold this time.

She followed me upstairs. Usually, whenever I'd walked up the wide, shallow staircase in Paradise End, I'd stopped and looked down over the banisters, lingering over the beauty of it all. I didn't want to this time. It was as if the enchantment that had held me had been broken.

I made Tia strip off her wet things and have a warm shower. I was restless while she was in the bathroom, moving round the room, going constantly to the window, watching the last of the cars drive away, and waiting for – I didn't know what. For something to happen, I suppose.

I was talking to Tia through the bathroom door, asking her if she was all right, when headlights from outside lit up the room in a garish glow. I ran back to the window. A big black car was coming up the drive. It stopped. The dazzling lights went out. Mr Hollins stepped out of it, and hurried into the house.

My heart skipped a beat.

Why's he alone? I thought. Why isn't Dixie with him?'

I was about to run out to the gallery and look down into the hall below, when I saw something else outside, the last thing I'd expected. Mum was hurrying up the drive under her bent, black umbrella, her old raincoat wrapped round her.

I suppose I knew then, at that moment, that something terrible had happened.

'Tia!' I shouted through the bathroom door. 'I'll be right back. I'm just going downstairs for a moment.'

Then I raced out of the room, half tumbled down the stairs, and stopped dead, face to face with Mum.

I forgot how angry she must be with me.

'Something's happened, Mum, hasn't it? Is it Dixie? Did she crash her car? Is she hurt?'

Mum put her arm round my shoulders and squeezed them.

'Where's Tia, Carly?'

'Upstairs. In the shower. She got wet. I made her change.'

'Take me up to her.'

I still feel guilty when I remember how I felt at that moment. I ought to have been filled with pity and dread for Tia, but all I felt was an awful kind of excitement. I was right in the middle of a great drama, a matter of life and death, and I know, if I'm honest, that in a horrible way I was enjoying it.

We reached Tia's bedroom door and went in. She was standing at the window, wrapped in a fluffy white bathrobe. And a blue light from the police car that had just pulled up outside was flickering on and off, on and off.

'She crashed her car, didn't she?' she said, in a high, little voice. 'Is she hurt?'

Mum went up and tried to put her arms round her.

'Just tell me, please, Mrs McQuarrie,' said Tia. 'Is my mother dead?'

I hardly saw Mum's tiny nod, but Tia did.

'No,' she said, shaking her head. 'It's not true. I don't believe it. She was here just now. It's not true.'

'It was the wet road,' Mum said in a trembly voice. 'It was at that sharp bend, just before the junction into Torminster. Her car must have skidded on the corner. It crashed into the big old oak tree there. Mr Hollins came almost at once, and dialled nine, nine, nine.' She swallowed. 'It was too late, Tia. There was nothing anyone could do.'

She stopped. Tia had started making awful little moaning noises in her throat. My stupid excitement had drained away and my heart was turning over. I didn't know what to do. I couldn't think of anything to say.

Tia was staring at Mum, and the colour was draining out of her face.

'How can they be sure? People don't just die that quickly. They haven't tried. The doctors . . .'

'Tia, there was nothing anyone could do,' Mum said again. Her hands were twisting in her lap. 'She can't have felt anything. You must hold on to that. She didn't suffer at all.'

'I tried to stop her going! She wouldn't listen. She never listened!'

'Tia,' Mum began again, but Tia had turned away. The mewing noise had turned into a wail.

'I'm alone. I'm all alone!'

I understood then, when I heard that terrible cry.

Her mother's died, I thought. Dixie was her mother, after all, and she's died.

'Oh, Tia,' I said, reaching forwards, but she had pulled away from Mum's and my outstretched hands and buried her face in the cushions, and the back of her head, with its tangle of long, damp, silken hair, was the loneliest thing I had ever seen.

19

I don't know how long the three of us were there, not speaking, in Tia's bedroom. At last, Graziella came in. She was crying noisily.

'Oh Tia, my poor little one! I have been looking everywhere for you!'

She bent down and tried to put her arms round Tia, but Tia didn't respond. She pressed herself further into the cushions.

Graziella moved back, looking unsure of what to do.

'Is so terrible, poor lady. Always she drink, drink so much. I tell her, no, think of your child. Think of little Tia. You are the mother. But she never listen to me. That stupid Otto is all she care—'

'Graziella.'

Mr Hollins was at the door, looking embarrassed and uneasy. He was beckoning to her.

Graziella jumped up.

'I know. I am coming. Why are you bothering me to lock up her jewels when—'

'It's OK,' Mum interrupted gently. 'Tia will be all right with us.'

It was a relief when Graziella had gone. Some of Tia's rigidity had left her. She let Mum hold her against her side. Her face was almost expressionless, but her hands were busy, tearing the tissue she was holding into tiny shreds. I wanted desperately to help her, but I couldn't think of a thing to say.

At last I heard a sound, and I looked up and saw Frost at the door. I thought he was going to say something to Tia, to come up and give her a hug at the very least, but his face seemed to have set like stone, and I saw in a sudden weird flash a picture in my head of the ice inside him, a lump of it, hard and cold.

He stepped back out of sight at the sound of footsteps approaching from the gallery. I heard someone say, 'Good evening, sir. Police,' and I recognized Dad's official voice. A thankful, safe feeling washed over me.

'Ah yes,' Frost said, his voice remote.

'You're Mr Braithwaite, is that right?' Dad went on. 'I'm really very sorry about – she was your sister, wasn't she?'

'Yes. My twin sister. Yes.'

There was a pause, then I heard Dad say, 'Is your niece – how has she taken it?'

'I haven't spoken to her yet.' Frost's voice was icy.

Dad cleared his throat.

'My wife's here, I believe. You probably don't know this, sir, but my daughter Carly, she's a friend of Tia's. She's brought her round to our house a few times. My wife seemed to think . . .' Dad seemed to be struggling against Frost's silence. 'Well, she thought Tia might need a bit of looking after.'

'Very good of you. Of her,' Frost said, as if he was thanking someone for lending him fifty pence, or offering him a lift. He sounded miles away, as if he was speaking to a person he could only just hear.

'There are certain formalities, I'm afraid,' Dad went on, sounding official again, and though I couldn't see the two of them I could imagine him standing there, his feet planted on the polished floorboards, looking strong and kind, taking charge, being the person who knew what to do. 'An identification will need to be made. No – not now. In the morning. I'm afraid I'll have to ask you to do it.'

'Of course. Naturally. Where have you – where is she?'

'They've taken her to the hospital in Torminster.'

Tia, who had now let herself sink nearer to Mum's shoulder, was listening too. She drew away and stood up. I didn't know what to do. I was desperate to be close to her. I stood up as well and took her hand and we went to the door together.

Dad and Frost turned and looked at us.

'Oh, Tia, love,' Dad said. 'I'm so sorry.'

Tia was looking at Frost, waiting perhaps for him to say something. He didn't even hold out his hands to her.

'I've put a call through to Geneva,' he said, as much to Dad as to her. 'Your father's there on business at the moment. They're contacting him. He'll call back.'

The telephone shrilled suddenly through the house. Tia's grip on my hand tightened.

'That'll be him now,' Frost said, moving stiffly towards the stairs.

I tried to pull away, to let Tia go with them, but now that she had hold of my hand, she was clutching it tightly, so we went together, following Frost down the stairs and into the library.

Frost put the telephone into her hand.

'Hello, Daddy,' Tia said in a quiet, dry little voice.

She listened for a while without saying much, then put the receiver down.

'He's coming,' she said. 'He'll be on the first plane tomorrow morning.'

And then her face crumpled. She dropped her head into her hands, and her shoulders began to heave with sobs.

I woke up very late the next morning. We hadn't got to bed till after five, when it was already getting light and the birds were singing so loudly they'd have kept me awake if I hadn't been so dead tired.

I rolled over and saw a strange shape in the bed opposite mine and a ripple of blonde hair lying across the pillow.

Who's that? I thought. Who on earth's in Lauren's bed?

Then everything came flooding back to me.

Usually, it takes hours for me to come to. I feel like a half-dead fish being pulled up from the bottom of the sea, and I won't speak to anyone unless I can help it. But that morning I was awake at once. I lay on my back, staring up at the ceiling, hardly daring to move in case I woke Tia too.

I'd been the one who'd asked her to come home with us. Frost had still been in a daze, hardly aware of what was going on around him. Graziella had tried to take Tia off to bed, but Tia had clung to me and said she couldn't bear to be on her own all night, so I'd said, 'Come with us then, Tia, please. You can sleep in Lauren's bed. We'll be together.'

Dad had nodded and looked at Frost.

'That's not a bad idea, Carly. Once the press get on to this . . .'

Frost seemed to shake himself awake.

'Good Lord, yes. They'll be here in droves. I'll send Hollins round with you.'

'There's no need for that,' said Dad, and I couldn't stop myself, in the middle of everything, feeling a spark of pride that it was my dad who was in charge here at Paradise End. He was the one telling them all what to do.

At home, Mum had given Tia a mug of hot milk and one of her sleeping pills, and we'd carried Lauren, who sleeps like a zombie, downstairs to spend the rest of the night on the sofa in the sitting room. My head had been so full I thought I'd never get to sleep, that I'd never be able to sleep again, in fact, but as soon as I'd climbed into bed I felt exhaustion sweep through me, like a flood trickling into every corner of my body, and before I knew it I'd fallen asleep.

I pulled my arm carefully out from under the sheet and lifted it to look at my watch. I stared at it, amazed. It was eleven o'clock in the morning.

I lay on my side and watched Tia as she slept, half wanting her to wake up and half dreading it. What was I going to say to her? What does a person say to anyone the morning after their mother's died?

I couldn't stay in bed any longer. Moving cautiously, avoiding the place where the loose floorboard always creaked, I got out of bed and tiptoed to the door. Once outside on the landing, I heard voices in the sitting room, so, still in my nightie, I went downstairs.

Mum was sitting on the sofa and Graziella was perched on one of the armchairs.

'Carly,' Mum said. 'Awake at last.'

'And Tia?' said Graziella. 'She is still sleeping?'

'Yes.'

I sat down on the sofa beside Mum. There was something I had to get out of the way. It couldn't wait any longer.

'Look, Mum, I didn't skip the dress rehearsal. I know that's what you've been thinking.'

She frowned at me.

'No. Sam said it was cancelled. You should have told us, Carly. You shouldn't have gone off to the party like that. My mother would have taken a strap to me for being so deceitful.'

I felt guilty, and that made me start to feel angry.

'OK, Mum, but Tia really needed me. Even if Dixie – if it hadn't all happened, she just had to have a friend with her last night. You wouldn't have let me go however nicely I'd asked you. You wouldn't understand.'

'You didn't give me the chance.' She was still looking annoyed. 'As things turned out, it was a good thing you were there. But it leaves a bad taste, being deceived. How am I going to trust you again?'

'Because you can!' I knew I was going red. 'Last night was a one-off. You know it was.'

She shuddered.

'I certainly hope so. I wouldn't want any of us to live through that again. OK, Carly, we'll draw a line under this. I suppose I'm glad, for Tia's sake, that she's got a good friend like you. Poor child. Blessed with all that money and cursed with such a sad life.'

I curled my feet up under me, tucking them into my nightie. There wouldn't be a proper row. The worst was over, I could tell.

'What's going to happen now?' I asked Graziella.

She shook her head.

'I don't know. Her father will say. Who knows?'

'But you'll still be there, at Paradise End, won't you, Graziella? She'll need you whenever she comes home.'

As I spoke, a cold feeling was beginning to settle in my stomach.

Graziella shrugged.

'Why will she come back here? Her father will take her with him to South America.'

'What do you mean, South America? She can't go there! She belongs here, at Paradise End!'

'Paradise End? If they have any sense in their heads they will sell it,' Graziella said casually. 'Is too big for anyone to live.'

I felt stunned, as if I'd been hit. Questions crowded into my head, but before I could say anything Dad walked in. He was in uniform.

'What's happened?' said Mum. 'I didn't expect you back till this evening. I thought you were on duty all day today.'

'I am.' Dad sat down on the other armchair. 'I've been up at Paradise End. Since I was passing I thought I'd look in to see how the girls are doing. You OK, Carly? Where's Tia?'

Mum got in first.

'Still asleep,' said Mum. 'Graziella's come to fetch her as soon as she wakes up. Her father should be arriving soon.'

Dad looked relieved.

'Good. He'll get Tia away from here, if he's got any sense. The press are swarming all over the place like wasps on a jam sandwich. We've had to put a couple of men on to keep order.'

'I suppose it's still chaos in the house?' said Mum.

'The catering people are clearing up.' Dad looked at his watch. 'I haven't been up there long. There's been so much to do this morning. I had to take the brother over to Torminster to identify the body.'

'Don't, Dad,' I said, shock tingling through me.

'Don't what?' He looked surprised.

'Don't call Dixie "the body" like that.' I could hear my voice wobbling. 'It's horrible. She was a person. I knew her. She was Tia's mum.'

'Sorry, love.' Dad squeezed my shoulder and I shook his hand off. 'Police jargon. I wasn't thinking.'

'How was he?' Mum said. 'It must have been awful for him, poor man.'

Dad shook his head.

'He's a cold fish. Looked down at her and said, "I confirm that this is the body of my sister, Deirdre Braithwaite," as if he was in court or something. Then he turned away. Funny thing, she could just have been asleep. Her face wasn't touched at all. She looked peaceful. Almost happy.'

Graziella sniffed.

'If she is happy it is for the first time since I knew her, poor lady.'

The phone rang.

'I'll get it,' said Mum, going out of the room.

She came back a moment later.

'It was Mr Hollins,' she said. 'Tia's dad's arrived. Mr Hollins is coming down here with the car to fetch her. I told him she was asleep, but perhaps we ought to get her up.'

I was just about to jump up and run upstairs to wake her when Graziella stood up.

'I will go,' she said. 'I brought her clothes.'

I sat back on the sofa again. Things were happening so fast I couldn't believe it. Everyone else was taking over, moving in on my best friend, pushing me out of the way. My throat was tight with misery.

Graziella was upstairs for a long time, and when she came down again with Tia, Dad had left and Mum was outside talking to Mr Hollins. The big black car was pulled up at the kerb.

Tia looked pale and heavy-eyed.

'Are you OK?' I said. I was feeling almost shy.

'I don't know. I feel weird.'

'Do you want me to go home with you? It won't take me a minute to get dressed.'

'No, Carly.' Mum had come back into the kitchen. 'Let Tia see her dad on her own.'

I wanted to kick Mum. I waited, hoping Tia would turn to me, like she always had done in the past, that she'd want me to be with her, to help her through. But Tia only nodded, and I felt as if a knife had gone into my chest.

'Yes. I'll go on my own. I'll call you.' Then she turned to Mum and said, in her polite-little-girl voice, 'Thank you very much, Mrs McQuarrie. It was very kind of—'

'Don't be silly, love.' Mum interrupted her with a

crushing hug. 'We're always here for you. You know that. You can come any time you like.'

She nodded, but looked as if she'd hardly understood.

'Come, Tia,' Graziella said. 'Your father is waiting for you.'

Tia drew in a deep breath.

'I haven't seen him for three years. I don't even remember what he looks like.'

'You'll be all right.' I felt shaky, as if I was going to cry. 'It'll all be fine. You'll call me, won't you? I'll be desperate to know how you are.'

She looked at me, and a smile wobbled in the corner of her mouth.

'I'll call,' she said and went out quickly.

Outside, Mr Hollins was holding the back door of the car open. Tia and Graziella got in, and he shut it behind them.

I stood there, watching the car drive off, up the short distance to Paradise End. I saw it push its way through the crowd of reporters who were hanging round the gates, and in my head I could still hear the bang of the car's back door as Mr Hollins had closed it on her. It was shutting them in and shutting me out, and I'd never been so miserable in the whole of my life.

20

'What's been going on? Why doesn't anyone ever tell me anything round here?'

That was Lauren sticking her nose in. Mum had sent her off to play with Francine all morning, to get her out of the way, but now she was back, and her sharp little eyes were snapping with curiosity.

For once I hardly noticed her. She was background noise, like the irritating buzzing of a fly.

'Francine's dad said the crash woke him up in the middle of the night,' she said. 'And it must have been really loud, because they live miles away. Did Tia cry a lot? Is she going to have to wear all black clothes and everything? Francine's dad says that Paradise End belongs to her now. Do you think she'll let me and Francine swim in her pool?'

I'd been trying up till then to blot out Lauren's irritating little voice, but I looked up sharply as I took in what she'd said. That Paradise End, or half of it anyway, would now belong to Tia was a strange, unsettling thought.

I drifted around for the rest of that afternoon, hardly knowing where I was, picking things up and putting them down and staring out of the window without seeing the rain that was still slashing down against the glass.

The phone kept ringing. The whole village seemed to have heard about the accident, and that the McQuarrie family were somehow involved. They all wanted to get the inside story. I dived for the phone every time it rang, hoping it was Tia, but it never was. In the end, Mum put the answerphone on. I ran to listen to it whenever a voice came through, feeling worse and worse every time it wasn't Tia.

There was only one message that mattered. Mrs Litvinov called to say that the dress rehearsal had been rearranged for Tuesday, the evening before the display. I was to be at Torminster Town Hall, with my costume, at seven-thirty. It didn't seem to matter any more. Dancing was a million miles away, part of another life.

At last, at six o'clock, when I'd given up hope of ever hearing from Tia again, she rang.

'Carly? Are you there?'

I couldn't speak for a moment.

'Hi, Tia. Are you OK?'

'Yes.' She sounded remote. 'Daddy's here. He wants to meet you. Are you still there, Carly?'

'Yes. How long is he staying? When do you have to go back to school?'

'To school? I'm not going back there again.'

I knew what was coming then, and my heart was sinking through my shoes, right down into the floor.

'Wow.' I tried to laugh. 'You'll have to go somewhere though. How about coming to mine? Torminster Comprehensive, here comes Tia.'

She didn't answer straight away. My eyes were squeezed tight shut as I waited.

213

'Actually, Carly, I don't think I'll be going to school in England at all. Daddy wants me to go and live with him in Argentina.'

I don't remember the rest of that call, only that Tia asked me to go up to Paradise End straight away. I got changed and tried to smooth my hair down and told Mum where I was going, and then I walked up the road. And all the time, churning around inside me, along with sadness, was a little dash of hope, that I'd got everything wrong, and that once I was there she'd tell me they'd decided to live in England and stay on at Paradise End after all.

I'd forgotten about the reporters, but there they were, just as Dad had said, crowding round the gates. I stood back, hesitating, not knowing how to get inside.

One of them saw me and said, 'Hello. You a friend of Anastasia's? How's she coping with all this? You weren't at the party last night, were you? Are they staying here? Was that Rudi Krukovsky who came in a while ago?'

'I don't know anything,' I said, thinking on my feet for once. 'I've got a message for my dad, that's all. He's one of the policemen on duty inside.'

'Oh.' The reporter looked disappointed, and another one, who'd lifted his camera, let it fall again.

Then I saw Mr Hollins behind the bars of the gate, signalling surreptitiously to me. He pressed the button and the gates swung open.

'Come to see your dad, did you say?' he said loudly, playing along with me. 'What's his name then?'

'Sergeant McQuarrie.'

'OK. You can come in. He's probably round the side of the house, on the terrace.'

I slipped in between the gates and they shut behind me. Mr Hollins turned his back on the reporters and smiled at me, and I ran up the drive and turned right in front of the house to go round on to the terrace.

Then, when I was about to lose my right to be at Paradise End, it caught at my heart again. The mess of the party was still around, the blackened torches, the half-dismantled marquee, the tables on the terrace where the buffet had been set out. But the house itself, *my* house, rose up above all that, serene and beautiful. I remembered my old childish fantasies, how I'd dreamed that I'd become a famous dancer one day, and buy Paradise End, and make it all my own. How childish and silly those imaginings seemed now.

I had to blink back tears and tell myself furiously not to be a fool before I could go on.

I'd only just reached the terrace when Tia appeared at the far end. She came to meet me. I felt oddly shy.

'I forgot to warn you about the reporters.' She sounded reassuringly normal. 'Did they hassle you?'

'Not much. Mr Hollins let me in.' I stole a look at her. She was steadier than I'd expected, but her eyes were red. 'How's your dad? I can't believe he got here so fast.'

'I know. He was in Geneva on business. Lucky he was so close. He got the first flight this morning.'

Neither of us could think of anything else to say. We sat down on the steps where we'd been last night with Rory and James. It seemed like months, even years, before. There was another long silence.

'Carly,' Tia said at last.

'What?'

'You're going to think I'm awful.'

'I won't. Try me.'

'I'm not entirely, well, not a hundred per cent sad. About Mimi, I mean. Not as sad as I ought to be anyway.'

'I don't blame you. She said herself she wasn't much good at being a mum.'

'I don't mean that I'm not sad for myself. It's not about me. It's for her sake. I've been talking to Daddy. He says she was always really unhappy, even when they were married, even when she was a child, I think. Daddy loved her, he said, but it wasn't enough. She ran off with someone, and then someone else, and they got stupider and stupider, like Otto. And she kept drinking too much. He says she couldn't help it. He says I shouldn't think too badly of her. She was just – I don't know – unhappy, I suppose.'

'Don't you think she'd have started being happy maybe, if she'd found the right person?'

'No.' Tia had been talking calmly, but now her lips began to tremble. 'She had me, but it wasn't enough. You know what she was like half the time. She didn't even notice that I was there.'

'But she loved you,' I said, trying not to sound uncertain. 'I'm sure she did.'

'Really? Did she really, Carly?'

I didn't know what to say. I was so sorry for Tia that the feeling actually hurt.

'My father said I ought to try to remember the good things,' Tia went on, 'but I couldn't remember anything much. Then he was looking in her desk, for her will or something, and he found – come on, I'll show you.'

We got up and I followed her through the long glass doors into the drawing room. It had been cleaned up since last night. The only reminder of the party was a stale smell of cigarettes and wine, and the bare mantelpiece.

Tia picked up an album lying on a coffee table.

'Go on,' she said. 'Have a look.'

I sat down on the nearby sofa and opened it. There were photos stuck on every page. Under them were captions, written in big, loopy handwriting, almost like a child's. They said things like: 'Tia and Mimi on the beach', 'In the bath', 'Tia's third birthday', 'Look, Mimi, I can dance!'

'Maybe you're right. Maybe she did care about me a bit,' Tia said. 'Once, anyway, or she wouldn't have kept these photos and written all that stuff, would she? Do you see, Carly? She wouldn't, would she?'

Her sea-green eyes were fixed hopefully on me.

'No, of course not. Of course she wouldn't,' I managed to say, but now selfish thoughts were pushing through to the forefront of my mind.

What about us, Tia? I wanted to say. *Do you want to stay friends with me now?*

She took the album out of my hands and shut it again.

'I've got to think about the future, about my new school in Argentina. It's a really nice one, my father says.'

Here it comes, I thought. This is it.

'That's great!' I could hear how insincere my voice sounded. 'You'll be back here for the holidays though, won't you? At Paradise End?'

217

My heart was thumping as I waited for her answer.

'I don't know.' She didn't look at me. 'We haven't decided yet what to with this place.' Her voice had lost its warmth and sounded almost detached. 'Daddy doesn't know if we can keep it on.'

'You're not going to sell it? You can't!' I couldn't stop my voice rising. 'Your family's always lived here. It would be – I don't know – wrong!'

She looked at me, frowning. I couldn't read the expression in her eyes.

'I used to hate it here when it was just Mimi and me and Frost. I was always lonely and miserable. I only started liking it when I met you. Then last night, when we were together at the party, before – it was so wonderful. I could see how it could be. How it was meant to be. Only it never was, because of everyone being so unhappy. Maybe one day, when I'm older, I could make it like that again. How do I know?'

I couldn't look at her.

'When are you going?'

'That's just it, Carly. Daddy wants to leave as soon as possible because of the reporters and everything. We're going to London for a few days and then straight back to Argentina.'

'Yes, but when?'

She looked down.

'Tonight. We're going to London tonight. Graziella's packing my things up now.'

I couldn't say a word. I was taken by surprise by the wave of anger, red and blinding, boiling up inside me.

218

'I'll go then,' I said, jumping to my feet. 'Goodbye.'

Tia looked up at me, startled.

'What do you mean? You haven't even met my father.'

'So what? He won't care.'

'He will! He does! I've told him all about you, about you being my best friend, and . . .'

She was looking upset now.

'Best friends?' I knew I sounded cruel, but I couldn't help it. 'Best friends? When I'm here and you're in South America? How, Tia? How?'

She looked as if I'd slapped her, but I couldn't stop myself.

'You'll be fine, won't you? It'll be great for you. New York, Buenos Aires, a nice new family. And I'll be stuck here, in this poxy village, with my boring, boring parents and my septic little sister forever and ever, amen.'

I couldn't go on, because I was crying.

Tia had taken a step backwards.

'And it's no good,' I managed to say, 'going on about us keeping in touch and all that because you'll never be back here. You'll never see me again. You'll make heaps of new friends, because you're so sweet and nice, and they'll all love you to bits. You'll forget about me the minute you're off through those gates. But I won't forget, not ever. I'll miss you for the rest of my life.'

And then I ran away. I just turned and bolted, dashing through the gates and the crowd of reporters so fast they didn't have a chance to even see who I was.

People get dumped all the time, I know they do. Boyfriends and girlfriends and best friends and mums and

219

dads – everyone dumps everyone. It doesn't make it any easier. It's the worst pain there is, I think.

I couldn't believe that Tia was going off like that, to the other side of the world, without seeming to care about me at all. And I couldn't bear to think that, from now on, the gates of Paradise End would be closed to me.

You used me, I kept saying in my head.

No one seemed to understand.

'Cheer up, love,' Mum kept saying. 'You'll have other best friends. There are plenty more fish in the sea.'

There was no one at school I could talk to. It was horrible because the newspapers were full of Dixie's death. The headlines said things like: 'Dixie in death crash', 'Suicide or accident?', 'Last fling for Dixie', 'Poor little rich girl loses her mum'. Everyone knew I'd been Tia's friend and they kept on and on at me, asking stupid questions, like, 'Did Tia's mum really rip all her clothes off and dance on the tables, Carly?' 'Is it true what it said in the *Sun*, that everyone was off their faces on cocaine?' 'What's it like, being at a real orgy?' 'Wow, you're so lucky, being friends with Tia. Why didn't you let us meet her too?'

I tried not to say anything, but I couldn't help losing my rag a few times. OK, so I know my temper's awful, and I've got a bad reputation for it, but it's got its good sides too. Everyone was scared I'd blow my top, and they shut up after a bit. As a matter of fact, I felt better when I was angry. It was worse being miserable, and that's how I felt most of the time.

On Tuesday, when I got home from school, a parcel was waiting for me.

'Graziella brought it this morning. She's going today,' Mum said.

'Going? Where?'

'Back to Italy. Mr Braithwaite's given her a lump sum, and she's going to set up a dressmaking business. She looked really happy. Go on, aren't you going to open your parcel?'

I took it up to my room. Lauren was there, so I had to go into the bathroom (the only place in our house where there's any privacy at all). I locked the door, sat on the bath and pulled off the wrapping paper.

It was Tia's best doll. She lay on my knees in her little black dress, with the rope of tiny pearls round her neck, staring up at me out of her sightless eyes.

There was a note tucked inside her collar in Tia's small, neat handwriting.

Dear Carly,

This is my best thing, so I want you to have her. She sort of belongs to you anyway, because she made you think about asking me to do your dress, which was the nicest thing anyone ever did to me.

You were wrong about me forgetting you. It's not going to be like that. You'll forget about me first, I know you will.

The funeral's on Friday, in London. Frost's trying to keep it quiet, so the press don't find out. I'm absolutely dreading it. I wish you were here. We're going to Buenos Aires on Sunday. I'll call you before then. If I don't get you, try me on my mobile.

All my love,
Tia

You'd think, wouldn't you, that I'd be pleased getting a lovely present and a letter like that, but I wasn't. It just made me feel resentful. It flashed into my head that the doll was like a payment, paying me off, as if I'd been a servant or something, and once I'd got hold of that idea I couldn't get rid of it. And then the letter made everything feel more final. I'd half hoped, I suppose, that Tia's dad would change his mind, that somehow they'd all end up staying on at Paradise End and it would go back to being like it was before. Now I knew for certain that it was all over, and that Tia was really going away.

'What did she give you to me for? I don't want you,' I hissed at the doll, giving it a shake.

The door handle rattled, making me jump.

'Carly?' said Mum. 'What are you doing in there? Come on out. You've got to get off to the dress rehearsal. I've ironed your dress. It's all ready.'

For the first time since Tia had gone, I was jerked out of myself. I'd actually forgotten about the dress rehearsal and the display and my dress. I'd even forgotten there was such a thing as tap-dancing. I couldn't think how I'd ever been keen on it. I couldn't imagine how I'd ever be able to do it again.

I don't know how I got myself down to the bus stop and into Torminster. On autopilot, I suppose.

The dress rehearsal was a disaster. My feet felt like a couple of wooden blocks stuck on the ends of my legs, and I couldn't dance a step. I tried not to catch Mrs Litvinov's eye, but when I did I could see her looking anxiously at me. She was worried that I'd mess up the display and let

222

her down. Part of me hated seeing the disappointment in her face, but part of me really wasn't bothered.

When I got home, Mum said, 'Tia phoned a couple of times. She wanted to speak to you.'

'Did she?' I said, sounding really sarcastic, although my heart had jumped up into my throat.

Mum looked at me closely.

'You two haven't quarrelled have you?'

'No, and it's none of your business,' I said rudely, and stamped up the stairs and slammed the door of my room so loudly it would have jerked anyone else but that little slug Lauren wide awake at once.

21

L ife's so weird. It's the night of the display and, would you believe it, I don't even care?

I have to be at the town hall early, so I take the bus into Torminster soon after five.

'Good luck, love,' Mum says, trying to kiss me as I go out through the door. 'We'll be along later. Reserve us some seats at the front.'

Lauren's coming, of course, and even Sam has decided to as well. Normally, I'd be over the moon, wild with excitement, tapping my feet as if they were drumsticks and the whole world was my drum.

In the dressing room the others are strung up like guitar strings.

'I know I'm going to be hopeless,' they say. 'Have you looked in the hall? They're arriving already. Feel my heart. It's pounding. Is my hair OK? Can you do my zip up at the back? I'm going to die, I know I am.'

I don't feel nervy like them. I feel a lump in my chest, that's all. It's not stage fright. It's not fear. The misery of the past few days, the rejection and the anger and the loneliness, are all coming together into a single word. Betrayal.

The word takes hold of my mind. It gets warmer. Little

flames start licking round it. That's what's happened. I've been betrayed!

It's anger that I'm feeling now, a new kind of anger, sharp and clear. It's spreading through me, hot and violent, making me tingle and sweat. It's running like fire through my body, down my arms and legs, into my hands and feet.

My feet! They've started to twitch. They're beginning to tap. They want to move, fast and furious, do what they like, go where they want. But I've got to control them. I must get the rhythm, channel the anger, get the music into my head.

Chick a boom, chick a boom, chick a boom di boom boom.

I've been waiting for hours. For some crazy reason, Mrs Litvinov's put me on at the very end, after everyone else. I feel I've been here forever when at last she sticks her head round the dressing-room door.

'Carly! You're on. Good luck!'

This is me, silk dress smooth, hair slicked down, tap shoes on my feet. I'm on the stage, the bare boards under me. People are out there, staring at me, but the lights are in my eyes and I can't see them. I can only hear their restless shufflings and coughings, and then nothing but the music as I start to move.

Move? I'm flying! I'm pounding those boards! I'm hopping and stepping and tapping, as fiery as the Tap Dogs, as smooth as Fred Astaire, my anger my fuel, my skill making it work for me.

Clickety clack, clickety clack, chick a boom boom da!

In my head, I hear Mrs Litvinov shout, 'Smile, Carly! Look happy!' And I do smile. I don't feel happy, not yet, but I feel powerful again, myself, with edges, stronger, in control.

The last drum beat crashes out. I come to a perfect stop. The audience erupts with claps and cheers. I peer out through the lights and see, of all people, Lauren in the front row, her face shining, clapping like a maniac, and Mum and Dad and Sam beside her.

I bow and turn to go. They're still clapping. I bow again. And then, out of the corner of my eye, on the far side of the hall, I see the glint of light on a head of smooth honey-coloured hair.

It's Tia! She's here! She's sitting at the end of the row, right on the edge of her seat, and she's clapping so furiously her hands are going like pistons.

I don't know how I get myself off the stage, but I do. Mrs Litvinov is waiting for me in the wings. She actually hugs me.

'I knew it,' she says. 'You brought tears to my eyes, Carly. There are a lot of things you can't do yet, but you'll get to the top if you want to. The sky's the limit for you.'

Any other time I'd have practically fainted with pleasure, but now I can't wait to get away. I say, 'Thank you very much, Mrs Litvinov. It's only because you're such a brilliant teacher. I hope your mum's feeling better,' and then I almost push her out of the way as I fly out into the hall where the lights have gone up and everyone's putting their coats on.

Tia's already gone down to the front of the hall and is standing in the middle of my family. There's a tall, slim man with a bald head there too. He's got to be her father.

She's the first of the group to see me, and she comes dashing up the aisle.

'Oh, Carly, you were so brilliant, I couldn't believe it. I've never seen anything like it. You were miles and miles away the best of everyone. And wearing the dress. I felt so proud I didn't know what to do. I wanted to stand up and shout or something.'

She grabs my hand and pulls me towards the others.

'Daddy, here's Carly. My best friend.'

Have you ever felt so happy you wanted to sing at the top of your voice, but with a kind of sadness mixed in that eats you up inside? That's how I felt that evening, after the display.

Everyone crowded round me and told me I was great, brilliant, wonderful, fantastic, a genius, except for Lauren, who said, 'I'm going to be as good as you. Miss Tideswell says.' And Sam, who said, 'I don't get it, Carly, what had those floorboards done to you?' The triumph of it all made my head feel light. But the best thing, better than the triumph, better than the praise, was knowing that my best friend had come.

'You got here! I thought you were in London. I thought you might have gone to Buenos Aires. I didn't expect you at all,' I said.

I wanted to tell her I was sorry, that I hadn't meant all the awful things I'd said last time we'd met, but I couldn't find the words. She seemed to have forgotten though, because there wasn't a shadow in her face as she smiled at me.

'I told you I was going to come, ages ago. Don't you remember? I promised you,' she said. 'Anyway, I couldn't have stayed away.'

'She dragged me here,' her dad said, nodding at me.

I don't know what I'd expected him to be like, but he was different anyway. For one thing, he had a foreign accent. Then he was quite handsome and young-looking, although he was bald, but not a bit like I'd imagined a multi-millionaire count would be like. I could imagine him with Dixie. They must have looked great together.

It was odd, but at that moment I almost missed Dixie.

Her cruel, selfish side that I'd always found so frightening was fading in my memory. All I could remember were the rare moments of warmth, and the flashes of radiance in her smile.

Tia didn't seem to notice that I'd gone quiet. She was saying something, but I didn't take anything in until she got to the last few words.

'. . . see you next year.'

'What?' I said. 'What about next year?'

She stepped away from her father and I saw the old anxious look in her eyes.

'Are you OK, Carly? I was just saying, you know, what we might do. I mean, I might come over to England in the Easter holidays or something, but if you'd rather . . .'

'Oh!' I turned to her eagerly. 'You mean you'd come back and stay at Paradise End?'

'No.' I held my breath. 'It's going to be let, till I've grown up anyway. I thought maybe – I mean, would you mind if I came and stayed with you? Just for a few days.'

Lauren overheard. Trust her. She grabbed Tia's arm and started jumping up and down.

'Tia's coming to stay, Tia's coming to stay!' she chanted.

'It'd be great,' I said, my sadness gone. 'If you know

228

what you're letting yourself in for. Have you quite finished, Lauren?'

'And then next summer, do you think – I mean would you like to come to Argentina?'

My jaw dropped. My eyes practically bulged.

'You have to be kidding, Tia. You really, really do. It would cost a fortune for starters. I'd never . . .'

'It doesn't have to cost you anything.' She looked embarrassed. 'We'd send you a ticket.'

My head started whirling round. I nearly said, 'Wow, would you? That would be so amazing.'

But then, I don't know why, an uncomfortable pride kicked in.

'I don't think I'd want that,' I said slowly. 'It might change everything. I might start feeling – I don't know – strange or something.'

'Oh!' She sounded upset. 'I didn't mean . . .'

I smiled. My head was steady again. I could dimly see that our friendship was going to change. It wouldn't be about Tia's need and my envy any more. We were going to find a new way forward, a more equal way.

'It's all right. I don't mean that I won't try to come. But if I do I'll pay for it myself. I'll get a job or something and save up.'

'Would you? Really?' She looked impressed. 'It would take you ages.'

'We've got ages,' I said, and the future suddenly looked different, more interesting, more serious and much, much longer. 'We're best friends, aren't we? And that means for life.'

*

Time's a funny thing. It plays strange tricks on you. It's nearly a year since Tia left England and went to Argentina. Frost moved out of Paradise End at once, and I don't think he's been back since.

They let Paradise End to a country club. The builders moved in again, but not for long. They didn't change too many things. If you walked in through the big front door, and looked to the left and right, into the red dining room and the golden drawing room, you'd think it was just the same, except for the reception desk in the space under the gallery, where there are telephones and notices on a board and there's always someone on duty.

The rooms haven't changed much except for a few small things. The china parrots have been taken out of the dining room, and so has the big table. There are lots of smaller ones there instead, usually set ready for a meal. Some of the pictures in the drawing room have been put away, and the precious carpet's in storage. There's a plain one in its place. The big grandfather clock at the foot of the stairs has been moved to a corner of the library, out of harm's way.

How do I know all this? Because I've got a weekend job there, that's why. It's a struggle, fitting it round my tap, but I manage it. Just. Mum says my homework suffers, but she's wrong. I squeeze more things in, that's all.

I'm working for Jepson's, who got the contract to run the catering services at Paradise End. I'm only needed when they put on big functions, and want waitresses or someone extra at the reception desk. There are weddings and parties most Saturdays, and on Sundays sometimes as well, so the money's piling up. I'm saving most of it for my trip to Argentina. I reckon I'll have enough by this time next year.

When I email Tia, I tell her little snippets about what's happening at Paradise End. 'The pink roses by the terrace are in flower', I write, or, 'They've put new lights round the pond. It's magic at night.' I don't tell her about how some of the books in the library have been nicked, and how her bedroom's been divided up into three small offices.

I don't tell her either that the spirit of Paradise End has changed. For a long time, Dixie's beautiful, wandering, cruel spirit seemed to linger in the rooms. It's gone now. Paradise End feels safer, even a little ordinary. Sometimes I remember how Tia and I slipped through its enchanted rooms on that beautiful, terrible night and I shake my head in disbelief. But I know it happened. I know what we felt. Then and now, Paradise End was our house, hers and mine, and it still is.

I tell her stuff about my life, when I write. Sam's gone off to college at long last, so I have his room in term-time. It's great to have my own space. Maybe that's why Lauren and I get on better these days, because she's not crowding me out the whole time. My tap's going brilliantly. I'm going for the county championships this year, and if I win – who knows? Mrs Litvinov says I could even try for a dance-and-drama scholarship when I leave school. She says why not aim for the stars? You can only end up on the ground, where you started from in the first place.

Tia didn't come at Easter. Her dad was ill and she didn't want to leave him. But a letter came from her last week, a proper one through the post, on notepaper with a fancy border. I've propped it up on the shelf in Sam's room and I read it whenever I go in. It says:

Dear Carly,

Guess what? I'm coming to England in July! Definitely this time. Daddy and Lucia are going to Austria, and I've persuaded them to let me stay in England instead. Do you think it would be all right if I came to stay with you? I don't want to be a nuisance, or be in the way or anything. Will it be OK? What would your mother say? I just can't wait to see you.

Frost's going to be in London. I'll have to spend some time with him. He almost never leaves Zurich now. Daddy seems to think he's become a bit of a hermit.

Give my love to everyone. Please say I can come. I can't wait to see you!

Lots and lots of love,
  Tia

The letter confuses me. I'm pleased and excited at the thought of seeing her, of course, but I'm nervous too. I'm afraid she'll have changed. Maybe she'll have become grand and posh, like the rich girl she is. Maybe I'll start feeling spiky and jealous, like I used to sometimes.

There's a photo slipped in with the letter. Tia's sitting on a fence somewhere in a garden. She looks great, with her hair tucked back behind her ears and a happy smile on her face.

But if I look closely I think I can see the old anxious questions in her eyes.

You still want to be my friend, don't you, Carly?

You don't think I'm totally useless? I can trust you, can't I?

Yes, I say, as I put the picture down again. It's OK, Tia. You can trust me. We're best friends, and that means forever.